# Carny:
# A Novel in Stories

### James Hitt

Aberdeen Bay

Albion - Beijing - Topeka - Washington, D.C.

Aberdeen Bay
Published by Aberdeen Bay, an imprint of Champion Writers.
www.aberdeenbay.com

Copyright © James Hitt, 2010

All rights reserved. No part of this publication may be reproduced, stored in a database or retrieval system, or transmitted, in any form or by any means, without the prior written permission of the publisher. For information on obtaining permission for use of material from this publication, please visit the publisher's website at www.aberdeenbay.com.

PUBLISHER'S NOTE

This is a book of fiction. Names, characters, places, and incidents are either the product of author's imagination or are used fictitiously. Any resemblance to actual persons, living or dead, business establishments, government agencies, events, or locales is entirely coincidental.

AUTHOR'S NOTE

International Standard Book Number
ISBN-13: 978-1-60830-040-2
ISBN-10: 1-60830-040-4

Printed in the United States of America.

*To my wife Vicki, whose encouragement kept the fire alive.*

Carny:

A Novel in Stories

# CHAPTER ONE

## Gazonie

At Warbling Brothers Road Show and Circus, we had our gazonie just like Ringling Brothers or Barnum and Bailey. All shows, big or small, had them. They were part of the business. You couldn't get away from them. It was the name we gave temporary laborers at the bottom rung of our world. Don't get them confused with the roustabouts, those permanent guys who we depended on day in and day out no matter what the situation. Those guys were family. But a gazonie was a pothead or a wino or an ex-con or just a general roughneck. Most lasted only a few days or a month until they made enough money to feed their habit, whether it was drugs or alcohol or women. For the most part, the crew or performers refused to associate with them because they usually meant trouble, some more than others, like this guy I'm going to tell you about by the name of Sojourn Parker.

Our winter quarters were just outside Richmond, California, up near San Francisco. Because we worked mainly California and parts of Arizona and Nevada, our winter was short, running from mid-November to early March. Sojourn Parker showed up in Spring of '48 just as we were getting set to go back on the road.

Old man Warbling and I stood by one of the trucks going over a stack of manifests when this guy came strolling toward us. The way he walked, crouching, his eyes shifting from side to side, I knew right away he was an ex-con, probably just released from San Quentin across the Bay. We often got ex-cons looking for either handouts or a job. We never gave them handouts, but those who wanted jobs wound up bedding with the gazonie, and like I said, most didn't last too long. But then every once in a while, one would surprise you and turn out to be all right. A couple stuck around long enough to join the roustabouts. So I didn't mind giving them a second chance, although I kept my hand close to my wallet and an eye on the cashbox.

"Here comes another one," Mr. Warbling said. He was sole owner of Warbling Brothers. He had no siblings, adding 'Brothers' to the show's name because he thought it gave us class. And maybe some might confuse us with the big boys like Ringling Brothers. Fat chance of that. We had a dozen rides, a circus with a dozen acts, a couple of sideshows and a handful of concessions, the kind of outfit that small towns hired for their Frontier Days or Fourth of July celebrations.

Every spring Mr. Warbling showed up to take stock of the show and give us our itinerary for the coming season. He didn't like ex-cons, but he let me hire them. A week before, he said to me, "Once a crook, always crook." He rolled up his left sleeve showing me an old, raised scar that ran from his wrist to his elbow. "An ex-con gave me that one night. We were traveling between towns, and he smarted off. I fired him on the spot. He pulled a knife, and the son-of-a-bitch carved me up along with two of the gazonie before the boys got him down."

"What did you do to him?" I asked.

"We beat the livin' shit out of him." The old man grinned. "We left him in a ditch beside the road. He was missing most of his teeth and his ribs were stoved in. A broken arm, a busted kneecap. Still, I figure he got off easy."

"How's that?" I asked.

"We didn't kill him."

"How do you know you didn't?"

"I never read anything about in the newspapers. A thing like that, a dead man in a ditch, that makes headlines."

Now here was another ex-con to deal with.

"We could still use a couple of guys," I said.

The old man chewed tobacco and spit. A thin ribbon of brown liquid ran down his chin, and with the back of his hand, he wiped it away. "You handle it," he said and wandered off in the direction of the pie wagon.

He came walking down between the trucks in a kind of swagger, carrying a valise so old and worn the handle had broken and been repaired with electrical tape. "You the boss?"

he asked. His voice sounded deep and hoarse like he gargled with gravel. I judged him to be in his mid-to-late thirties, but I could have been wrong about that. His left eye drooped, and his nose seemed to go in two different directions at once. He stood a good six feet in height, and even though he wore a baggy shirt, I could see he had plenty of muscle under there, but his skin appeared sallow from too many years out of the sun.

"How long have you been out?" I asked.

He appeared mildly surprised I recognized him as an ex-con. "Half a day. As long as it took to walk from there to here."

"You looking for a hand out or a job?" I asked.

"Which you willing to part with?"

"You work the rest of the day, you get food tonight. You hire on, it's ten dollars a week. We supply grub and a place to sleep."

His eyes looked beyond me to guys breaking down tents and packing trucks. "I never worked for a carnival."

"It don't take a college degree to move things from one place to another." I waited while he thought on it, but after a few seconds I got impatient. "Yes or no?"

He rolled his shoulders in a shrug. "I'll take the job."

I called Dali over. He handled the crew responsible for assembling the rides. He was a good kid, not much past twenty, and one of the brightest guys who worked for us, but he stood barely five feet and a huge hump rose out of his back, forcing him into a crouch as he walked.

"What's your name?" I asked the ex-con.

"Parker." He smiled. "Sojourn Parker."

"This is Dali." I nodded to the kid. "You'll work with him."

Parker shot a glance at the kid, and his mouth twisted like he tasted sour lemon. To his credit, he said nothing.

Dali looked up at me. "A gazonie?" he asked, and I nodded.

"What's a gazonie?" Parker asked.

"A newcomer," I lied. "A guy who's never worked carnies."

"Interesting word." Parker's smile widened. "Words always interest me. You know, what they mean and what's behind them."

"Come on, I'll show you where you can store your gear," Dali said.

He started off, but before Parker followed, I said, "One more thing. You cause trouble, you're gone. You clear on that?"

"Yeah, sure," he said in an offhand way that irritated me. Right then and there I wanted to take back my offer, tell the bastard to get lost, but I made a bargain and I would stick to it, at least until he gave me cause to fire his ass. He must have guessed my reaction, and he said, "I won't cause trouble. I did my time. I'm a changed man."

"Seeing is believing," I said.

For the rest of the day I didn't give Sojourn Parker much thought. The job of getting ready to go on the road consumed all my time. When I wasn't checking the loading of the trucks, I fielded questions from old man Warbling. At one point he asked about Parker. "So what do you think of that ex-con you hired on?"

"Jury's still out," I said.

The old man spit, spewing a wad in the dust. "I gotta ask myself what's a guy hiding when he smiles all the time."

"Maybe he's just good natured," I said.

"Like hell." The old man wiped his chin with the back of his hand.

That evening I asked Dali how Parker had done on the job. "Okay, I guess. But he doesn't like taking orders from me. Maybe I can't blame him for that."

"Did he give you any lip?"

"He did his work. Afterward, I showed him where to bed down. I left him at the pie wagon. He seemed grateful enough. Maybe he'll work out."

I sensed a reservation in his voice. "What it is?" I asked.

The kid grimaced, shaking his head. "It's in the tone of his voice when he would say something to me, like he was mocking me." Dali shrugged. "Look, Boss, maybe I'm too sensitive. Maybe I'm reading more into this than he means."

"Keep your eye on him," I said. "Any trouble, you come straight to me."

Later that night as I lounged in my trailer listening to AMOS AND ANDY, I heard shouting from the gazonie tent. Every once in a while, one of those guys got drunk and caused a commotion. Cursing, I pushed myself out of my chair and went outside, intent on quieting them down. Even before the trailer door closed behind me, the night once again turned silent. Maybe I should have gone on over and checked things out, but I was tired. I went back inside, settled into my chair and upped the volume of the radio.

The next morning I was at the pie wagon having breakfast, and across the way sat this wino we called Tripp because he was so clumsy. Thin as a piece of old string, he reminded you of Icabod Crane. His left cheek was cut, his lower lip crusted with dried blood. His left eye was swollen shut. He noticed me staring at him, and he looked down at his food.

Finished eating, I got up and went over. "What happened, Tripp? You have too much to drink last night?"

His head moved in what I took for a nod. Tripp wore clothes so old and ragged they looked like Salvation Army rejects, his one valued possession an ancient watch with a cracked crystal and a face faded with time. He wore his sleeves rolled up, and I saw the watch missing. I figured he traded it for a bottle of Ripple. "You able to work today?" I asked.

"Sure, Boss." His lips barely moved.

"Lay off the hooch," I said. "I can't use a guy who's soused."

By mid-day, we tore down the last of the tents and packed them in the trucks. Our first destination was Oxnard, a little berg sixty miles up the coast from LA. In those days, it boasted a population of no more than two thousand, mostly farmers and ranchers. That was a long drive from Richmond, so we caravanned over to Oakland where a train waited for us.

We arrived at the freight yard just past four that afternoon, and by eight, we had the trucks and personnel all aboard. But we waited and waited, sitting on a side track watching trains arrive and depart, all coming from or heading north. Just before eleven, a conductor came to explain that on the other side of San Jose, a freight derailed when it collided with a melon truck. We were stuck here while the railroad cleared the mess.

Starting with the performers, I spread the word and told

them to get as much sleep as they could. That was asking a lot considering the hard seats. We were a small outfit compared to Ringling Brothers or Barnum and Bailey, and when we hired a train, we got second or third best. But my people were troopers, and they might grumble, but they would make do.

Working my way from car to car, I came at last to the flatcar on which rode the gazonie. Some already slept, curled up in balls, thin blankets thrown over them to keep the chill off, but four huddled at the far end, and I heard a voice say, "Raise a dime."

I jumped up on the platform. Right away the guys threw down their cards or tried to hide them in their laps. They knew the rules against gambling. Not that I had moral qualms against it, but in a working environment where you saw these guys every day, it could cause hard feelings, and hard feelings have a way of getting out of control. Problems like that I don't need.

Only Sojourn Parker failed to show any anxiety at my sudden appearance. With a smile, he glanced up, then threw a dime in the pot plus a second dime. "See you and raise," he said.

"There's no gambling. You boys know better than that." The other three looked away, not wanting to meet my gaze.

"Just a friendly game." Parker gestured to an empty space next to him. "Sit and join us if want, Boss. This game's open to everybody."

"Close the game or you're fired," I said.

The other three tossed their cards in the pile, climbed to their feet, and shuffled away. Parker's smile grew wider. "I didn't know you felt that way, Boss." Raking in the discards, he shuffled them until he straightened the deck and slipped the cards in his shirt pocket.

Standing, he stepped in a little too close, maybe trying to impress me with his bulk. I was three inches shorter and probably sixty pounds lighter, but I stood my ground, my hands on my hips. "The cards come out again, you're gone. Understand?"

We stared at each other until he said, "Sure thing, Boss."

I spent the rest of the day sitting around waiting for news that the tracks had been cleared. I hated times like that.

People with nothing to do can find all sorts of ways to get themselves in trouble. Sure enough, along about one-thirty in the afternoon, a gazonie fell off the flatcar and broke his arm. A yardmen drove him to a hospital, but the guy never made it back. Not that I expected him to. If I could, I would have turned our people loose for a while, but no one knew when the train would be moving out.

Well past midnight, more then a day and a half after we arrived at the yard, we were given the green light. The cars rattled and shook, and we were rolling. South of San Jose we passed overturned boxcars and a locomotive pulled off the tracks and lit by floodlights and welding torches. Pieces of broken melons lay scattered over the ground like cracked skulls.

After that, I scooted down in my seat, my head lolling against the cushioned rest. I awoke when Dali dropped in the seat beside me. Sitting up, I rubbed my eyes. Outside it was already light. I glanced at my watch. Six-thirty.

"We got trouble, Boss,"' he said. "This Sojourn Parker has got the gazonie scared out of their wits. Seems for once Tripp didn't fall and hurt himself. Parker wanted his watch, so he took it. And the guy who got taken to the hospital--he talked back to Parker. Parker twisted his arm until it snapped. Those guys back there are afraid of him. I'm thinking I'm a little afraid of him, too."

"He needs his comeuppance," I said.

Dali nodded. "That he does, Boss."

"You stay here." I rose and stepped across to the aisle.

In the third car back rode the roustabouts. Most were asleep, but not the Irish brothers, Sean and Fergus O'Malley, fraternal twins who, except for their red hair, shared few physical characteristics. Sean stood not much over five-six, but he was the toughest little monkey I knew, often taking on guys twice his size and beating the living crap out of them. Fergus was a large, hulking man with the biggest pair of hands I ever saw. They stood at the rear of the car waiting for me.

Fergus reached up for two pick ax handles on the rack above their seats, handing one to his brother. They always carried them for such emergencies.

Fergus slapped his open palm with the ax handle.

I stepped past them, and they followed.

At that point, we were along the coast just north of Ventura, the mountains on the left, the Pacific on our right. Between us and the water, a long slope ran down to Highway 101 where three or four cars, braving the early morning hours, headed south in the direction of LA or north toward San Fran. A heavy mist rolled in from the sea, and on the flatcar, men huddled in their threadbare clothes trying to find some protection from the wet cold. Parker sat with his back to us, and he never saw me till I stepped in front of him. With a crooked smile, he stood. "What's going on, Boss?" he said.

"You're nothing but trouble." Behind me the wheels of the flatcar clattered so loudly that I had to shout to be heard.

He raised one eyebrow, the smile fading. "These bums been talking about me? You know you can't believe a word they say. Maybe I should have a talk with them. Straighten 'em out." Then, with a voice hard and cold as glacier ice, he said, "You don't think I know what a gazonie is? I knew even before I signed on, but that was all right with me. I know how to handle these guys."

"You're through talking," I said. "Time to get off."

"You shouldn't say something like that--Boss." He grunted my title so that it sounded more like a threat than respect. "Look how close you are to the edge. A misstep, and you could fall between the cars. I mean--if that happened, they'd be picking up pieces of you all along the tracks."

He never bothered to look around, supposing, I guess, I was dumb enough to face him alone. I nodded to the two Irishmen. Parker's eyes widened in sudden understanding, and he started to turn when the first ax handle wielded by Fergus crashed between his shoulders. Right behind came Sean's blow. Parker collapsed in a heap, his butt crashing against the hard wood of the flatbed. He listed to the left, but before he toppled, Fergus scooped him under one arm, Sean the other, lifting him to his feet.

The O'Malley brothers stepped to the edge of the flatcar, and with one heave, sent Sojourn Parker flying into space. He hit the slope in a cloud of dust, going head over heels all the way to the bottom where he lay still, rocks and dirt piling on and around him.

I turned to the gazonie who stared at me in wide-eyed

wonderment. "Did you guys see that?' I said. "He was so drunk, he fell off the train."

At first no one said anything, but then one of the guys laughed. Soon they were all laughing.

At that point you might think the story ends. Not quite.

By noon the next day, we were set up in Oxnard for the weekend. Things went smoothly until mid-day Saturday when a Highway patrol car pulled up. A couple of cops climbed out of the front, and from the back emerged Sojourn Parker, his left arm in a sling, his face full of cuts and bruises, dark sand ground into his skin. He limped along behind the cops.

I went to meet them. The older cop, a big man with a protruding belly, said, "This guy says you threw him off a train. He wants to file a complaint. What do you have to say about that?"

I scratched my head like I didn't fully understand. "Well, I'm glad Mr. Parker's all right--at least, as good as can be expected. But, as far as us throwing him off the train, he's got that all wrong. He had just gotten out of San Quentin, and I guess he was celebrating a little too much. He got pretty drunk and fell off. You can ask anybody here. They'll all tell you the same thing."

The cop turned on Parker. "You didn't tell us you was an ex-con."

"You know, you're damn lucky," I said to Parker. "I mean--the way you were staggering around, you could've fallen between the cars. Why, if that happened, they'd be picking up pieces of you all along the tracks. Now if you want to come back--you know, if you want your job back--we'll have another go at it." I smiled good-naturedly.

"This son-of-a-bitch--" Parker began.

With a hand to Parker's chest, the burley cop cut him off. "You say another word, and I'm going shove my stick up your ass. You got a lot of nerve dragging us out here like this." To me he said, "Sorry for bothering you. You have a nice day now."

They left Parker standing with me and drove off. I said, "If you're not out of town in the next half hour, you're never leaving. The O'Malley boys will see to it."

"You're worse than anybody in stir," he said.

"We're carny people, and nobody fools with us." I waved my thumb at the road twenty yards away. "Get missing."

"They were only gazonie," he said.

"Yeah," I said, "but they're our gazonie."

CHAPTER TWO

Cocoa

I first saw her on an overcast May morning as our caravan rolled through Thousand Oaks.
In those days, the town was one long street with a few stores, a half dozen bars and a single motel. As in most small towns, when Warbling Brothers Road Show and Circus arrived, employees and customers alike came out to see us pass. Some waved but most stared at us like we were aliens from Mars.
Just before we reached our encampment, a vacant lot at the east end of town, we passed her sitting in a car. I rode shotgun in the lead truck that carried the Ferris wheel, and as we passed, she looked up without smiling, and if she noticed me, she gave no indication. Why should she? I was a gangly eighteen-year-old boy who had left home to join the carny. I wasn't anybody special.
But she was. I saw that right away. She had a beautiful face, a softly brown Madonna with big, ethereal doe eyes. I had seen those qualities in a few movie stars--Ava Gardner and Gail Russell. Maybe Gene Tierney in *Laura*. Whatever those women had, so did she, and I think right then I fell half in love with her.
We parked the trucks, all fifteen of them, and the boss came over to Bub and me as we stood beside the cab waiting for him. He always picked out the spot for the Ferris wheel first, and we built the midway around it. Bub and I were responsible for putting it together, and we could assemble the ride in less than a day and take it down in half a day.
The boss took a survey of the ground before pointing to a flat spot near the highway.
I grabbed one of the ropes, beginning to untie it, when the girl I had seen in the car came up to the boss.

"You took long enough getting here." She couldn't have been any older than me, and maybe a year or so younger, and she was even prettier up close. Her dress showed cleavage, but she still had plenty covered up. She pushed dark, curly hair from her forehead. "I've been stuck in this lousy town for three days. I was on my way to meet you in Lompoc when my car broke down. I sure hope you got a job. I'm broke and hungry."

"You're not another damn fortune teller, are you? I've had enough of them."

"You have a girls' show, don't you?"

Every carny had a girls' show, although rubes referred to it as hoochie koochie.

The boss scratched the side of his face, his fingernails scraping against his stubble. "I don't know," he said. "You're pretty light-skinned, but where we travel, the rubes don't take to nig—"

"My father was Iranian, my mother Irish." Her voice took on a defiant, almost angry tone. "I can fit in anywhere. Look-- what do you run--'Artists and Models', 'Paris Showgirls'?"

"The Shah's Harem."

"Even better. I'm a natural for that." Still the boss remained tightlipped, not quite ready to commit. Three weeks before, one of our girls left for a burlesque show that offered better money and less traveling, and ever since, he grumbled about needing a replacement. Now here she was, a gift from heaven. So I knew the boss would give in.

"What do they call you?" the boss asked.

"Cocoa."

"Well, Cocoa, you have the weekend to show me what you got. You see Mac. He runs the hoochie kooch. He'll set everything up for you."

The boss walked on to the next truck, at which point the girl noticed me for the first time. Holding a long iron pole, I stood staring at her like a lost puppy. "What are you looking at?" she asked.

Embarrassed, I felt my face turn hot. I could talk to most people, including the girls in 'The Shah's Harem.' I was no inexperienced, tongued tied kid. But she turned me into one. "I--I'm glad you got the job," I said.

"Yeah? And why's that?"

I shrugged and tried to find words that wouldn't embarrass me further. "You--well, you--you seem like a nice person," I said.

Her features relaxed, and she gave me a soft, throaty laugh. "You're a nice kid," she said.

My embarrassment turned to irritation. "I'm no kid. I'm eighteen, and you're no older than me."

"Honey, I'm a thousand years older than you," she said.

A hand slammed against the hood of the truck, and Bub, his round face screwed into an angry ball, said, "Stop gawking and let's get to work."

We opened Friday afternoon, and like most of the roustabouts, I worked a second job. In this case, I ran the basketball booth. Of course the balls were weighted to one side and the hoops were smaller than regulation, so no matter how good the rube was, he had little chance to bring home the big prizes.

The booth sat directly across from 'The Shah's Harem' where bannerlines showed girls in skimpy costumes and a fat, middle-eastern sultan reaching out with both hands. The show really didn't start till later in the day when we had more adults than kids. I did pretty good business until Mac began his spiel, and then people deserted me to listen to him and watch the come-on.

With the handle of a cane, Mac tapped the microphone so that it sounded like drum beats that echoed down the midway. "Step right up, gents. Come in close. Get a good look at what's inside." He swept off his straw hat and waved it at the bannerlines. Off stage, our three-piece band struck up 'Song of Araby'. A crowd appeared to assemble as if on cue, mostly men and teenage boys, many, I suppose, who waited most of the day just for this. The tent parted, and out came Cocoa. The sun had dipped below the Santa Monica Mountains, but a ray of light crept through a distant pass, and like a heavenly spotlight, settled on her.

Mac turned back to the microphone. "Princess Araby, straight from Arabia and the shah's harem. She's going to give us a little sample what she did for the sultan himself before she escaped to the U S of A."

Cocoa began her dance, and it was easy to see why Mac made her the come on. If she was out front, what was inside? Her hips seemed to move independently of the rest of her, and the men and boys couldn't take their eyes off her, some staring at her crotch, others at her breasts or ass. In reality they could see little. All the important parts were covered--the boss wasn't about to give the local law a chance to raid us for indecent exposure--but she showed enough to arouse their imaginations. As she glided first right, then left, she looked at the rubes as if urging each to come on in and spend time with her. The drummer struck a symbol once, twice, three times, and each time, she shot her pelvis toward the audience.

Mac picked out a young man near the stage. "Watch out there, young fella! We don't want you to get hurt!" The kid jumped back to the raucous laughter of the crowd.

The boss had worked his way to my booth to get a better view. He must have seen me staring at Cocoa--how could any normal guy not help staring at her?--and he said, "Don't let her get to you, kid. The only thing she can give a guy is trouble."

"I don't want anything from her," I said.

"Hell, kid, we all want something from her, and she knows it." He turned his attention back to the stage. "I have to admit she's good. I guess I'll have to hire her."

"That's enough, Princess Araby. You don't want to give it all away for free." Mac waved his straw hat as Cocoa ran off stage. "That's only a sample, gents. The real show's inside, a bevy of beautiful girls wanting and willing to please. All for twenty-five cents, a mere quarter for a million dollar show. Beauties gathered from royal harems of the East, and all yours if you're old enough to buy a ticket. Only two bits. Come on in." Then in a deep whisper, he added, "We won't tell."

We planted a shill in the audience who made a big deal of rushing the ticket box and plunking down his quarter. "I ain't going to miss this!" He made sure to say it loud enough that everyone could hear. That jump-started the flow of men and boys willing to pay their quarters. They wouldn't see much. We had four girls including Cocoa, and each would do a sexy little dance without ever removing one stitch of clothing. From what I had seen of Cocoa, she was better than the others. Sapphire and Diamond, both slender, moved with a certain amount of grace, but Sheba was overweight and downright clumsy, stomping around the stage like a plow horse. The rubes didn't mind. The girls had a way of making them feel they were witnesses to an unknown but exotic world.

An hour later, the boss relieved me for supper. I was plenty hungry, and the cooks dished me out a plate of food and a cup of java. When I went to find a seat, I saw Cocoa by herself, finishing up her plate. She was still in costume, a flimsy robe wrapped around her, and she looked up when I stopped in front of her. "I saw you from my booth. You were great," I said.

"It's only a job. Nothing special."

"I've seen a lot of others, and you're better than any of them." I offered her a smile, but she remained religiously stoic. My face began to heat up, and I started to move away.

"What's your name?" she asked.

"Bobby."

"Sit down, Bobby. Hell, it's been days since I've talked with anybody, really talked with them. So talk to me. Tell me something."

"What'd you want to hear" I asked.

She shrugged. "How did you find your way here? Start with that."

So I sat and told her my story. It wasn't much of one. After I graduated from high school, I worked for a local gravel pit company doing back-breaking labor for twelve hours a day and hating every minute of it. When Warbling Brothers came to town, I caught carny fever and moved on with them. "My mother wasn't too happy. I think she would've kept me home. My stepfather didn't give a damn. Actually, I think he wanted me gone. We never got along."

"Stepfather." She spoke the word with deep bitterness, and her face turned dark. "Looks like you and me have something in common."

After that we talked every day, mostly about the show and the performers and the roustabouts and the rubes. We never again talked about ourselves, not really, but that was fine. Sometimes she didn't feel like talking at all, and we would sit together until she was ready. That was fine, too.

At night I lay in bed, my hands pressed together, my

mind conjuring up images of her, the way she tilted her head just so, her soft smile she reserved only for me, her lips ripe and full, her milk chocolate skin smooth and inviting to the touch. Sometimes when her image wouldn't let me sleep, I took myself out to the midway where we kept the lights on all through the night, even when no one was around, and I read books I picked up along the way. I didn't have many, but I loved KING SOLOMON'S MINES and TARZAN, and I held a special fondness for an old yellowed copy of IVANHOE, which I read over and over again. I often pictured Cocoa as the sensual Rebecca, the woman with whom Ivanhoe should have ended up.

  The day I knew she liked me, really liked me, we traveled from Santa Susana to Covina, and she rode with Bub and me in the cab of our truck. Most of the drive, she leaned into me. I suppose that was partially because Bub carried an extra sixty pounds and smelled a little rancid from sweating all the time. Still whatever the reason, she excited me. I tried not to show it, and I looked out the window a lot to keep my eyes off her, but she must have known.

  By then she had become the star attraction of the hoochie kooch, and rubes often came back a second or third time just to see her. The boss ordered a new bannerline for Princess Araby, the Concubine of Potentates. I wasn't sure the rubes knew what 'concubine' or 'potentate' meant, but the bannerline looked impressive and offered all sorts of delights if the guys were willing to part with two bits. The boss even gave her a private dressing room, although it was little more than a partitioned off corner of the hoochie kooch top after we assembled it in each town. She let me come back there, too, and I brought her java or supper or whatever she needed. She liked that, but I think it worried her, too, because one day just after we set up in San Jacinto, she asked, "What the hell you want from me, Bobby?" The question came as a surprise, but I can see now she must have been thinking about it for a while. "Men always want the same thing, and I suppose you're no different. Maybe you're just more patient."

  I dipped my head, staring at my feet. "I like being with you. I like talking to you."

  "Talking only goes so far. Sooner or later, you're going

to want more."

"Is that so bad?"

"Most of the time it is," she said.

"I'd never hurt you. Never."

Her expression turned hard, what my mother would have called brittle. "I've heard that before, Bobby. I've heard it too many times."

"But I mean it," I said.

"Yeah, you probably do. Maybe they all meant it." She sat at her dressing table, staring at herself in the mirror, which was streaked with dirt so that the diffused light from outside cast a halo around her face. She shrugged. "We'll see."

The next day I was working the basketball booth, while Cocoa danced on stage and Mac gave his spiel. The rubes crowded around the bandstand as she glided around and shot her pelvis at the audience. Then she ran off stage, and the line formed for tickets. That was when this woman holding a little boy's hand stepped in front of my booth. I started to tell her the kid was too little to shoot the hoops, but before I got a word out, she said, "That woman who was just on the stage. Where can I find her?" She spoke with a deep Texas accent.

I judged her to be in her late forties, maybe early fifties, and she wore her wrinkles like a badge of honor, no makeup, no effort to disguise them, her hair rolled into a tight bun. Her dress was fifteen years out of date, hanging loosely all the way to her ankles. The little boy, no older than three or four, was dressed in clean pants and a pressed shirt, his hair slicked back and combed. I took her for one of those religious nuts who occasionally came to complain that we were all sinners damned to hell unless we changed our ways. I thought she decided to work on Cocoa. "Well, ma-am, you see we aren't suppose to give out that information," I said. "Now if you would like to see the boss--" I pointed up the midway, intending to direct her away from the hoochie kooch where she could cause less trouble.

"That's my daughter." She scrunched up her face in such a way I thought she was about to cry. "I want to see Barbara. I want to see my daughter." I was too shocked to answer and stared at her like a deaf mute. Finally, she said, "Come on, Tommy. We'll find her ourselves." She and the boy headed off for the entrance, then bypassed it and went toward the rear.

Regaining my senses, I released a flap that dropped across the front of the booth announcing it was temporally closed and hurried after the woman and kid. I caught up to them as they pushed their way through the rear of the top.

Cocoa sat before her mirror. Turning, she stood as the woman led the child into the dressing room. I followed standing just behind them, bracing myself for trouble if it came.

"I saw you in the crowd," Cocoa said. "You shouldn't have come. It won't do you any good."

Out front the three-piece band began to play the intro for Sheba, the first act. Cocoa still had a good fifteen minutes before she wrapped up the show.

The old woman held out the boy's arm as if she expected Cocoa to take it. "You need to do what's right."

"Right?' Cocoa uttered a laugh completely devoid of humor.

"You need to come home," said the mother. "I need you home." She looked down at the boy. "He needs you, too."

Cocoa put her hands on her hips, casting a quick glance at the boy before concentrating on the mother. "And what about Silas Meechum? Does he need me, too?"

The mother's shoulders slumped. "He's gone," she said.

"So he left you?"

"Yes, but not in the way you think." The mother spoke so softly I had trouble hearing her. "He's passed on. A cancer in his lungs." The mother held out a liver-spotted hand to her daughter. "Please, Barbara, just come home."

"Why the hell should I? I got a good job here. I make good money. I got nothing back there."

"You got us." The mother coughed, covering her mouth with a fist. She cleared her throat. "It's best you come. The boy is going to need you."

Cocoa's eyes went wide with surprise. She opened her mouth to speak, but only a sharp breath escaped. "We been looking for you for over two months now," the old woman said. "We ain't got any more time, and we ain't got any more money. We'll be going now, going home. You decide to come, we'll be waiting."

The old woman and the boy turned and started past me when Cocoa said, "Wait." I saw the anguish in her face.

She reached into her purse, pulled out a wad of bills, and rushed to the old woman, who took the money, well over a hundred dollars, looking at it as if she thought it was about to burn her fingers. "I'll take it for the boy's sake," she said and stuffed the money in a pocket. Without another word, she and the boy shuffled out of the dressing room.

Cocoa watched them disappear before her attention shifted to me. "Don't you say a word to anyone about this, you hear?" she said. "I don't want anybody knowing my business. I don't want you knowing it. So just keep out of it. Don't say a damn word."

Ten minutes later, the band began to pound out the music for her act, and she went on stage and performed as if nothing had happened, her face and body never once betraying her feelings, whatever they were.

I didn't say a word, not then, not ever. As she said, it was her business, none of mine, no matter what I felt about her.

And what good did my silence do me? None.

Two weeks later she was gone. She packed her one suitcase and crept off in the night without any one noticing. She didn't even leave a note.

I never saw her again, though every time I heard of another carny show I asked if anyone there knew of her. If she joined one, she may have changed her name. Or maybe she went the burlique circuit.

Of course, one other possibility existed. She may have returned home to take care of the mother and boy. I hoped so. But the more I considered that possibility, the more easily I saw myself for who I was, seduced and deluded by romantic illusion. What the hell was I thinking? We were carny people. There were no angels in our business, only fools and knaves, and I knew which category I belonged to.

## CHAPTER THREE

## Fake

The moment I saw Angel, I knew she would be trouble. Women always are. We set up in a vacant lot right in the middle of Personville, a border town about thirty-five miles east of San Diego on Highway 12. You probably never heard of it, and for good reason. It ain't there any longer. Or rather, the falling-down buildings are there, but the people have moved away long ago. But in those days, the town had a reputation as being wide open, and you could find just about anything you wanted, including whores and gambling and enough marijuana to keep the whole state high for a year. Once each June the town celebrated their version of Frontier Days to try to fool people into thinking it was a family town, but everybody knew how crooked it was. It had been that way since the 1920's.

We had just tightened the last bolts on the Ferris wheel, and the crew and performers broke for supper. We didn't have anything to do until ten the next morning, a Friday, when we opened for business. Our routine seldom changed. We worked a three-day weekend, and on the following Monday, we would tear it all down and move on to the next town where we would set up again. It was a routine we were all familiar with, and things ran smoothly, except when they didn't.

And that's where Angel comes in. I first spotted her as she parked her pickup and got out. She was dressed up in her gypsy outfit, although I could see from her fair skin she wasn't no gypsy but just trying to look the part. We was sitting around the pie wagon having lunch, and she stopped at the far end and asked Dali a question. Dali was a hunchback with this big flat nose and thick lips, but she didn't flinch one bit when she looked at him, and I liked that about her. Sure enough,

Dali pointed to me, and I thought, Damnit, I'd just like one meal without people butting in.

She strolled over, holding up her long skirt so it didn't drag in the dust. I sat there chewing my food and looking pissed off, but that didn't bother her either. "My name's Angel Farrell. I'd like to join your outfit."

She had eyes like Bette Davis. You know, the ones that look like they're about to pop right out a person's head. Despite that, she wasn't bad looking, and even though her dress was baggy, you could tell she had a good figure. Still that's no reason to hire a woman. I laid down my fork and knife. "What's your schtick, honey?"

"I can see the future."

I shook my head in disgust. "I thought so. A damned fortune teller."

"I have my own setup." She pointed to a small area next to the funhouse. "I could put down right over there. I wouldn't be in anybody's way."

"Who were you with before?"

"Smith and Prescott. For three years."

Smith and Prescott were larger than us, but they worked Arizona and New Mexico and sometimes West Texas. Our paths never crossed, but I heard of them. Their reputation was solid enough. And carny people were always moving around changing jobs, and the fact she stayed with Smith and Prescott so long was a good sign. Still something about her bothered me. Maybe it was the way she stared at me with those big eyes. "Why'd you quit?" I asked. She didn't answer right away, and I said, "Well?"

"Sometimes people don't like what I see."

"You're suppose to tell 'em what they want to hear."

She laughed without making any noise. "You think I'm a fake," she said.

"Honey, we're all fakes," I told her. She started to say something else, but I waved my hand, silencing her. "Tell me why I should hire you."

"People like having their fortunes told, and I'm good at what I do." She must have seen the doubt on my face, and she said, "Look, I'll set up for the weekend and split the profits 50-50. After that, if you think I'm worth it, you can sign me on."

"Sixty-forty. I get the sixty."

"You get it?"

"Yeah, me." I pointed a finger at her. "But the first sign of trouble, you're out of here. Understand?"

"Sixty to you," she said. I could see it plain she didn't like me. Like I gave a damn. I figured she'd been out of work for a couple of weeks and didn't have much money, so she had to take pretty much what I offered. "And I should be grateful?" she said.

"Take it or get missing." I went back to my food as if she wasn't there.

She took all of ten seconds before she caved. "I'll get my stuff."

She walked back to her pickup. By ten that night, she had her tent erected and a big banner with red lettering proclaiming: "MADAME SUZOTSKI KNOWS ALL, SEES ALL, TELLS ALL," and under the words, a silhouette of a woman with a crystal ball, and under that "$1."

We opened the next day, and everything went smoothly, just the way I like it. The crowds started showing up around noon, and by evening, the place was packed with rubes. The Ferris wheel developed an irritating squeal, as it often did, but we paid it no mind. Hell, if that was all that was wrong, we were having a great day. Sure enough just past midnight when the last customer dragged himself home and I counted up the receipts, we cleared nearly a grand, a damned good sum for opening night. Saturday would be even better.

I was in my trailer finishing the receipts when Angel came in and dropped a wad of bills on the table. Before I could open my mouth, she said, "I'm not holding out on you. That's sixty percent of my gross, just like we agreed." I stated to ask how much, and again she beat me to the punch. "Forty-four dollars."

I swept the bills off the table and stuffed them in my pocket. "You're not going to count it because you trust me," she said.

"Like hell," I said.

She smiled. Frankly, she didn't look half bad when she smiled. "That was a joke. I can see you don't trust anybody."

"You got that right, sister." I pointed her toward the

door. "Go on. Get out. I got work to do."

"Don't I get a 'thank you?'"

I glared at her until she shrugged, turned and left, still smiling. Then, just when I thought I was rid of her, she paused at the door and looked back. "Trouble's coming." I didn't bother to answer because I figured she was trying to spook me. Trouble was always coming in our business. "It's a badge," she said.

Of course it was a badge. We were always having problems with cops. So what? "Get the hell out of here," I said.

The next day was big just as I thought it would be. By noon we must have had close to five hundred people riding the rides, playing the booths, wandering through the funhouse. Our circus, which had ten acts including jugglers, a bareback rider, and high wire flyers sold out for the first performance, and that seldom happened. Things couldn't have been better.

Then just past noon this guy showed up. I picked him out right off, even though he wore a suit and let his wife and three kids tag along behind. His jacket hugged him a little too tightly, and I spotted the bulge under his left arm. And he had this thin scar that ran from his temple to his jaw. At first I took him for a local tough. He went straight to the ticket booth and asked Becky a couple of questions. Next thing I knew he was coming my way followed by his whole brood.

"You in charge here?" His voice was gruff, like he was used to giving orders and having people follow them. I nodded, and he said, "You know who I am? I'm chief of police of Personville. I'm here to make sure you're running a clean show."

"Yes sir," I said with a smile. "Glad you came. Everything clean and wholesome. Family entertainment." I led them back to the booth where I grabbed a roll of tickets. There must have been a hundred on that roll. "Compliments of Warbling Brothers."

He took the tickets, tearing off half a dozen at a time and handing them to his kids. His wife stood behind him silently watching with hang-dog eyes. Her hair was frazzled, and her faded house dress hung on her skinny frame like a shapeless potato sack.

They wandered off into the crowd, and I felt pretty pleased with myself. The law had shown up as it always did, and I had taken care of things like I always did, smooth and friendly-like. Sure, it was going to be a great day, a hell of a day.

And then an hour later, I seen the whole family go into Angel's tent. Before I could get too worried, Becky called me over to the ticket booth. Becky was an older gal, matronly if you want to know the truth, but I could trust her better than most with the money. I doubt she skimmed more than five or ten dollars a day, and I never once caught her, which says a lot right there. Guy had passed her a fifty dollar bill, and she knew not to give change till I took a look. I held the bill to the light, snapped it a couple of times and saw it was legit. After that, I went back to strolling the midway, making sure none of the rubes put anything over on us while we was putting things over on them.

He found me at the rubber duck booth--you know, the one where little rubber ducks with colored plates on their backs float around a tank while rubes throw nickels at them. Different color dishes netted different prizes. The red dishes were the biggest and best prizes. We oiled them so they was slick, and the nickels slid right off into the water.

At any rate, the chief was madder than hell. I could see it in his face, all red and full of steam. He looked like he was ready to hit somebody, and that somebody was me.

He stepped in close. "I got enough to shut you down right now. You hear? Shut you the hell down!" He screamed the last words, and the people near us stopped chattering and playing the ducks to look at us. A few began to edge away.

I held up my hand and backed off a step. "What's wrong, Chief? Give me a chance to fix it. I'll take care of it."

He punched me in the chest with a big forefinger. "That damn Ferris wheel sounds like its about to fall apart. That's enough right there."

"Hey, come on, Chief. It just needs a little oil." Then something came to me like a voice from heaven telling me it wasn't no Ferris wheel that got him so riled. "What's bothering you, Chief? You tell me, I'll fix it. You got my word."

He grabbed my arm and pulled me a few feet away so we was all by ourselves and no one else could hear. His fingers dug into my flesh just above the elbow, and it hurt like hell.

"Your goddamned fortune teller. That's the problem." He clenched his jaw, and the anger grew more fierce, and his grip on my arm tightened, sending shock waves all the way to my fingertips. "I should run her in. I should run all of you in--"

"Chief, Chief--" I pulled at his hand, but he refused to let go. "I'll get rid of her. As of right now, she's gone. I swear. I don't owe her a thing. She only joined us yesterday." That appeared to mollify him some, and he eased up on the grip, finally letting go altogether. "I'll take care of it right now. Send her packing."

As I stepped around him, I noticed his three kids, a boy and two girls, none older than ten, wide-eyed as they stared at their dad. I didn't dwell on that. I went straight to Angel Farrell's tent. She was already in the process of packing her glass ball and tablecloth in a small trunk. She stood and faced me.

"What the hell did you say to him?" I asked.

She looked me square in the eye. "I told him the truth. I told him what I saw." She gave a depreciating laugh. "You're right. I should learn to lie. It would serve me better."

"The truth? What the hell you talking about?"

"I told him to get out of the deal he was making. That if he didn't, his black heart would be stopped by a heart blacker than his."

"His black heart--? What the hell does that mean? Are you trying to ruin us?" I didn't really want answers. I was angry and scared. If that bastard shut us down and word got around, pretty soon no town would have us. I wanted her gone, and this whole thing over. "I knew you was trouble when I first saw you. I knew it. I knew it."

"I'm packing," she said, her voice filled with resignation.

"Not fast enough." I kicked the table, the leg crackling and the whole thing suddenly tilting.

An hour later she had her tent down and tossed in the bed of her pickup. She came back one last time for her iron stakes, and I was waiting.

"You want today's cut." She held out her hand with twenty-one dollars. I snatched it, and our hands touched. Her head jerked like she felt a little electric shock, and her eyes

widened.
    She was trying to spook me again, but I wasn't buying it. "Go on, git," I told her.
    "You know, I'd feel sorry for most guys if what was about to happen to you was about to happen to them. I wouldn't tell them anything. I wouldn't want them worrying and trying to stop what they can't stop. But you--you I'm going to tell."
    I crossed my arms over my chest and leaned against the corner of the funhouse. "Well lay it on, sister, and see if I believe a word of it."
    She squatted and gathered up the last half dozen stakes. They clattered together like warning bells. When she stood, she said, "That left arm of yours--use it while you can. Pretty soon it's going to give you lots of trouble."
    "You've got me shivering in my boots." I shot a thumb toward her pickup. "You've had your say. Now let me see your dust."
    Two weeks later, we were in Indio, and I read in the local paper that a couple of hikers out in the middle of the Mojave Desert stumbled on the body of the police chief of Personville. The buzzards and vermin had gotten to him, but there was enough left to see that somebody had put a bullet in the back of his head first.
    That same weekend, I was having a couple of beers at a bar, and for no reason other than I told this loudmouth to keep the noise down, he pulled a knife and cut me pretty good. Took over a forty stitches to close the damage, and my left arm was in a sling for more than a month. It's a little stiff to this day, especially when it rains.
    Makes a guy wonder, don't it?

## CHAPTER FOUR

## Acquaintance

We were an hour from closing when he showed up. As usually happens, the traffic at the ticket booth had slowed to almost nothing. Under the circumstances I get bored, so I bring a book along. A couple of times the boss complained about me reading on the job, but he knew I never stole a penny from Warbling Brothers Road Show And Circus. Before I came, the ticket takers skimmed money every night.

The booth was cramped, and I held the book against the grate to catch the light from the midway. That was when he stepped up to the window with two dollars and a big smile.

Irritated, I laid the book aside. He looked to be ten years younger than me, which would have put him near thirty, but what set him apart from our other male customers was that he wore a shirt and tie. He didn't wear a jacket, but that would have been foolish considering this was late June in Indio where during the day the temperature seldom drops below a hundred. Even the night remained hot. By then, I must have looked a sight. My hair was frazzled, and the little makeup I applied that morning had melted away long before noon.

As he handed me the bills, he nodded toward the book at my right hand. "Pretty steamy stuff for such a hot night." He had a slight lisp when he pronounced his 's's'.

I tore off twemty tickets and slid them forward. Ordinarily people don't bother talking to me, so I didn't have much practice at small talk. He took the tickets and looked quickly over one shoulder, then the other. "These are for my nephew. Little guy's wandered off." He waved a goodbye. "You have a good night, Miss. Enjoy that book now."

He strolled off down the midway in search of his nephew. As it turned out, he was my last customer of the night.

About half an hour later I saw the young man once more as he stood near the entrance looking the place over. The midway was practically deserted, but I guessed he still hadn't found his missing nephew.

I returned to my book until fifteen minutes later when knuckles rapped on my door. I slid the lock and swung the door outward. There stood the boss waiting for the receipts, his left arm in a sling. As usual I had stacked the bills by denominations, wrapped them with rubber bands, and dropped them in a cloth sack with the loose change. With his one good hand, the boss took the bag and shook it a couple of times to judge the weight. "Not much here, Becky."

"One customer the last hour." I reached under the counter for my purse and slipped the paperback inside. The boss took a couple of steps back to give me room to exit, but he didn't offer his hand.

"Hope you didn't skim too much off the top." His mouth turned up in a smirk. "Slow night like this--not much profit as is."

As bosses go, he wasn't bad. He paid us on time, and he didn't get drunk very often. For the most part, except when he was mad at somebody else, he seldom yelled at me. But he was always kidding me about pocketing money from the till. The first couple of times I was offended until I realized it was only his little joke.

"We'll have a better day tomorrow," the boss said. "Saturdays are always better."

About a block down just off the highway sat The Wild West Bar and Grill. My throat was as dry as the desert, and I wanted nothing more than a cool beer. I probably should have walked straight to my trailer and gone to bed, but the thought of that beer proved too tempting.

With my purse in hand, I sat off. The show kept its lights on all night, and plenty of cars flew by on the highway, so the way was well lit. Once a car slowed, the driver honking his horn and giving me the once over, but when I didn't pay him any mind, he sped up and disappeared down the road.

A single woman, even one as old as me, entering a bar can raise all sorts of eyebrows, but since Gus died, I had learned to cope on my own. I pushed my way through the door and found the bar full of smoke and men drinking. A couple of women sat with the men, making me the only unattached female in the place. I found an empty table against a wall and sat there for a good ten minutes before a waiter sauntered over and asked if I would like anything. I ordered a draft, and waited while he filled a frost-cover glass and brought it back. Passing him a dollar, I told him to keep the change. He didn't bother to thank me.

Before I could raise my glass, he was beside the table looking down at me, that big, friendly smile plastered on his face. "Good evening again. I just saw you sitting over here, and I thought I'd come over and say hello." Once again I noticed his trouble pronouncing 's's.'

He had loosened his tie and opened his collar, but wet patches discolored the underarms of his white shirt. He held a Bud in one hand, and with the other, he touched the back of the chair opposite me. "Mind if I join you? All the other tables are taken, and frankly, I don't know a soul here."

I glanced around the room, and sure enough, all the tables had filled since I came in. Still, I felt a little nervous letting a man who I didn't know sit with me. After all, he might get the wrong idea and think I was a loose woman. Then I asked myself who I was kidding? I was more than ten years older and built like a fireplug. A young, good-looking man like him would never make a move on me. Those days were long gone.

Still before I could answer, he seated himself.

"Did you find your nephew?" I asked.

His eyes widened in mild surprise. "Why yes I did. Thank you for asking. He lives just a couple of blocks from here. I dropped him at home than came here for a little refreshment before I head down the road. Hot days like this make a guy thirsty." He took a long drink, and when he lowered the bottle, he said, "You been with the carnival long."

"Ever since my husband died six years ago." I sipped the beer, not really wanting to talk about Gus. I still missed him. Not all the time like at first, but at night alone in my trailer.

His smile faded, and I thought he was about to give me some condescending platitude about death. Instead he said, "I lost my wife about a year ago. At times it hurts so that I wonder if I can stand one more minute."

Up until then, I thought he was a one of those lonely men who needed the attention of a woman, any woman, and he singled me out because I was the only one available. I was right about the lonely part. The poor boy had lost his wife just as I had lost Gus. He looked away and coughed once, but it sounded more like a sob.

He seemed to shake off his depression and faced me, a smile once more lighting his face. "I'm sorry. I shouldn't burden you with my troubles. Let's talk about something else. Let's talk about you."

"Not much to talk about. I'm a middle-aged woman working for a cheap carnival."

"You're not middle-aged. Why, you're not any older than my sister." He reached across the table and patted my hand. "She's only two years older then me. Why, you even look a little like her--but you're prettier, of course."

Suddenly embarrassed, I looked at my beer and tucked in a piece of errant hair behind my ear.

He said, "It must be exciting. I mean--working for a carnival. Lots of traveling."

I found little humor in his naive view of my world. "It's a job. That's all it is. And as for as traveling--" I lifted my glass and gestured around the room. "--we hit all the great cities like Hemet and Thermal and Indio. The highlight of most of my nights is crawling into my trailer and curling up with a book. Tonight is special. I came here for a beer."

"But you have a lot of responsibility. You handle all the money."

"Which the boss collects every night before I leave the booth." I took a sip of beer, but by now in the heat of this place, it had gone flat. "He doesn't trust a soul, including me. He's always accusing me of siphoning money from the receipts. I know he's only kidding, but once in a while, I think he actually believes it."

His smile faded and his brow furrowed into ridges. "Your boss is a real bastard to treat a lady like that. Why for two cents--" His face turned suddenly red, and he said. "I'm sorry. I usually don't cuss like that--"

Before he got the wrong idea, I said "For the most part he treats me fair."

"But he takes the money from you--"
"Every night at closing time. Before I can even get out of the booth, I have the receipts ready, all wrapped up just like a present. He's like a child that hoards his candy and is afraid one of his friends will steal it. Really, that's all he is. A child. But most men are."

"Still, he shouldn't treat you that way." I heard genuine sympathy in his voice.

We talked another five or ten minutes about nothing in particular, and when he said his goodbye and took his leave, I thought: Now there goes a young man any mother would be proud to call son, a nice young man who respects women.

When I returned to my trailer and climbed into bed, I felt warm all over. It wasn't often in this business you meet such nice people. Usually you meet grifters and hobos and general riff-raff, people who took advantage and afterward tossed you aside like old tissue paper. For some idiotic reason, I cried a little before I fell asleep and cursed myself for a foolish woman. Like most people, I felt life had given me far less than I deserved. But then, who gets everything they want? Only people in fairy tales.

I awoke the next morning suffering a slight depression, but I had only that one beer, so I couldn't blame my moroseness on that. By ten I was once more in the booth, a half dozen people already lined up for tickets. I met them with a smile, but it wasn't sincere. I couldn't shake the blues, and as the day grew hotter, the walls of the booth closed in like the jaws of a furnace. Sweat rolled from under my breasts and down my back. It plastered my hair to my head. Twice the boss sent people to relieve me, once around two for lunch, again around seven for supper. By then I was a wilted flower. The customers kept coming and buying tickets by the handful, and that helped to keep my mind occupied.

Just after eight thirty, the sun dropped behind the mountains, and the heat cooled enough to make the booth more bearable. Around eleven when the crowds began to disperse, I separated the day's receipts, bundling the bills in stacks of twentys, tens, fives and ones. We raked in so much that day that I put the loose change in two other bags.

Just after midnight, the last stragglers, a couple of

teenage boys, wandered off into the night, and right after, the boss knocked on the door. I grabbed the sack of bills and slid back the lock. When I opened the door, he was smiling. "Big day, Becky. The rubes were out in force today." He held out his good hand. "Well come one, let's have it."

I passed him the sack, and just as he took it, a voice off to the left and out of sight said, "Give me that money." The boss started to look in that direction, and the voice said, "Keep your eyes to the front, Mister. I got a .38 pointed right at your gut, and I ain't afraid to use it." The voice had a pronounced lisp.

The boss stood rigidly upright, frozen like an ice carving. A hand came out of the darkness and relieved him of the money sack. "You turn around in the next few seconds, and I'll blast you to hell." The hand and money sack disappeared, and the boss and I stared at each other as footsteps retreated in the gravel.

"Son-of-a-bitch." The boss spit the words between his teeth.

He called the police, who showed up with flashing lights. They asked all sorts of questions, but neither of us saw the thief. We didn't even know for sure he had a gun, only that he said he had one. A thin, wiry policeman who looked like Buster Keaton with a mustache shrugged and said, "Without a description to go on, finding this guy ain't going to happen." He seemed unconcerned, I guess because we weren't town folk.

"We lost maybe two grand. And there's nothing you're going to do?" the boss said.

"If I was you," said the cop, "I'd change my routine. Get a gun. Have two people pick up the receipts. Hell, it's your carnival. Do whatever you want." With that, he and his overweight partner got back in their patrol car and drove away.

The boss yelled after them, "Bastards!" They were more than half a block away, well out of hearing.

I never did tell the boss I met a fellow with a lisp. After all, I had just met the young man the previous evening, and I didn't know much about him. Since the boss was always accusing me of skimming from the till, it wouldn't be much of a stretch for him to think I had a hand in the stickup. I had seen him jump to conclusions plenty of times and then wind up being wrong. A couple of times his mistakes cost people their jobs.

And, too, I saw only a hand, never a face. I'd hate to condemn a young man on the strength of a voice that sounded familiar. And the more I thought about that weekend, the surer I became that I made the right decision. The way I saw it, that boy deserved the benefit of the doubt. After all, he was so polite, so thoughtful I just couldn't bring myself to believe he had a hand in this sordid mess. I've known lots of rotten men in my time, and I pride myself I can spot that kind a mile away. He just wasn't that kind.

I never did see him again, even the next time when we set up in that town. Yet seldom a week passes when I don't think of him. He was such a sweet young man.

CHAPTER FIVE

Musclehead

The Trailways bus pulled into Starkville, California, just past four in the afternoon, depositing me and my one small suitcase in front of Ma's Diner. If you've ever been to Starkville, especially in the middle of June or July when temperatures average 110, you know what a hellhole it is. The moment I hit the sidewalk, a blast of heat struck me in the face like scalding sand.

I hadn't eaten since early morning when I forced down a bowl of oatmeal, and my belly grumbled with hunger. In my pants pocket, I hoarded four dollars and a few pennies, the sum total of my private fortune, but I was so hungry that I took myself into Ma's and ordered a T-bone, mashed potatoes, and biscuits and gravy all for $1.75. Considering the toughness of the steak, Ma overcharged me, but at least I walked out of the place with a full belly.

After that, I went looking for Warbling Brothers Road Show and Circus, encamped west of town, their Ferris wheel towering above any of the buildings of Starkville. I stood in line at the ticket booth holding my suitcase and got curious stares from some of the rubes. When I reached the front of the line, I asked the middle-aged woman behind the cage where I could find the boss. She frowned as if she thought I might be trouble, but she directed me to the pie wagon beyond the midway. "He usually catches an early supper right about now," she said.

The pie wagon was a flatbed truck from where the cooks distributed meals to the workers and performers. The boss was easy enough to spot. He sat by himself at the end of one of the long tables, shoveling food in his mouth. "I'm a magician, and I'm looking for a job," I said.

Chewing his food he looked me over. "Who'd you

work for before?"

"Starrett and Floto."

"As a magician?"

I could have lied, but one phone call and he would have discovered the truth. "They already had a magician. I sold tickets and worked as a roustabout."

He pushed his plate back and picked up his coffee cup, appraising me over the rim as he drank. When he laid the cup down, he said, "And you came here because?"

"I didn't get fired, if that's what you mean."

"Okay, you didn't get fired," he said.

I guess I could have left it there, but I thought it best he knew the whole truth. "I was on my break when a signal 25 came over the loudspeaker. There was a commotion at the hoochie-koochie. I got there first, and found a drunk pawing one of the girls. Had her costume ripped half off. I laid into him. Turns out, he was a local cop's son. The boss thought he could keep things under control, but only if I hit the road. I heard you were going to be here. I want a chance as a performer."

Once more he gave me a long look from head to toe. "How much you weight? I figure one forty soaking wet."

It was a strange question, but then most bosses I'd known were strange in one way or another. "One forty seven," I said.

"And you think you can fight?"

"I have black belts in judo and Aikido."

"Black belts? What the hell does that mean?"

"It means I'm pretty good," I said.

He considered that for a few seconds while he sipped his coffee. Finally he said, "We got a magician. Been with us for over five years."

I knew that coming here was a long shot, but still I couldn't help feeling disappointed.

"I may have another job, if you're interested." The Boss pointed to the east end of the midway where I could see a bannerline, a long canvas strip that showed two men in tights, one holding the other in a hammerlock. "We started an athletic show about three months back. You know what that is?"

Anybody who hung around carnies knew about the Athletic show. The carny employed some muscles-heads who challenged all comers to a wrestling or boxing match. The show made its money from the rubes who paid admission to see their local boys perform against professionals. The boss said, "We lost a guy about a month ago. Got busted up pretty bad. He ain't coming back."

"And you want me to take his place?"

"I'll give you one three minute bout tomorrow morning. After that, we'll see."

They let me sleep in the tent with the roustabouts, and the next morning the boss marched in and tossed me a pair of wrestling tights that turned out to be a perfect fit. "Belonged to a tightrope guy who took a tumble," he said. "You're on in half an hour. Try not to embarrass us."

In truth I had never been in a ring. When I was stationed in Japan right after the war, I studied judo and aikido and competed in tournaments, but they were always formal and circumspect. When I stepped into this squared circle, I looked out on a half-full tent of loud-mouth rubes anxious to see their boy rip into me. I guess I should have been nervous, but I remained calm and focused, even when I looked across at my opponent, a big ranch hand who outweighed me by sixty pounds and stood a head taller. He kept looking at me like I was a wishbone he was going to break in half.

We got the instructions from the ref, an off-duty town deputy hired by Warbling Brothers. Professional wrestling rules applied--no eye gouging, no hitting below the belt, no tossing over the top rope. A win came by a pin of a three count or submission. We shook hands and took our opposite corners.

At the bell, he rushed me. You perform Aikido by blending with and redirecting the motion of the attacker, using his momentum against him, and I simply let the guy reach me, then I rolled him over my hip. He crashed into the mat, the wooden planks shaking under my feet like an earthquake. Twice more he came at me, twice more with the same results. Angry and frustrated, he pushed himself to his feet, and with lowered head, charged like a wounded bull. I stepped to the side, gave him a slight push in the back, and he slammed head first into the turnbuckle. He fell backward, all dead weight. I dropped on top, pressing his shoulders to the mat, but that was unnecessary. He was out cold. I stood, the ref held up my hand in victory, and I heard a scattering of applause. Two of the ranch hand's friends, one who cast a malignant glance toward me, climbed in the ring and helped their fallen comrade to his feet. The ranch hand was bleary-eyed and couldn't focus, but he wasn't hurt.

Ten minutes later back in the dressing area, the Boss found me. "You're next match is in forty-five minutes. One of the guy's friends wants a shot at you. This time, see if you can make it look a little harder. It's three rounds. Give the rubes a show."

The word had gotten around Starkville, and most of the town showed up. The guy's friend came at me more slowly, trying to intimidate me with his bulk, all the time sporting this crooked smile. I let him push me around for the first round, but in the second he tried to knee me in the groin. Right then I took him down with a leg lock, and he was slamming the canvas in submission.

For the next three weeks in three different towns, I entertained the rubes wrestling against local boys, sometimes as many as six or eight bouts a day. The show had two other muscleheads beside me, and they got their matches, too, but soon the boss gave me top billing as Killer Kane, the Beast from the East. When I stepped into the ring, the crowds booed, even though I never once resorted to a dirty trick. It didn't matter. It was me against them.

About two months after I joined Warbling Brothers, we set up in Lompoc, and by then we played to capacity crowds. I was about to go on for my last bout of the day when the Boss came to me with this big blond kid. "This is Russell. You two will go three rounds. Russell will bounce you off the ropes, you'll come flying at him, and he'll duck. He'll catch you coming off the opposite ropes and slam you for a pin. You got that?"

The kid sported a goofy smile and kept nodding like Lenny from OF MICE AND MEN. The boss slapped him on the back, and the kid left still smiling.

When he was gone, I said, "I'm suppose to lose? I can beat him. You know I can. I haven't lost a match yet."

"This ain't about winning or losing," the Boss said. "This is about money. Always has been, always will be." He took out a roll of bills and peeled off a ten spot handing it to me. "He paid twenty for the privilege. You get ten, the show gets ten. That's fair, ain't it."

I saw then the boss was right. Win or lose, we got paid a percentage of the gate. Now I got a percentage of the bribe. I slipped the bill in my wallet. "Sounds fair to me," I said.

Such a set up didn't happen often, but whenever it did, I went along and took my cut, telling myself it wasn't like a real fight. Money was the only object here. I lived with that reasoning for over a year, during which I threw half a dozen fights.

By then we were back in Starkville.

Midday on Saturday, the Boss came back stage with this guy who looked familiar but at first I couldn't place him. He had a girl with him, but she waited outside. She was a pretty redhead, probably no older than sixteen or seventeen and built a lot like Rita Hayworth, all delicious curves that invited all sorts of lascivious thoughts. "This is Billy Bob. Tonight it goes three rounds. You come off the ropes, he slams you for the count."

Billy Bob flashed a crooked smile, and then I recognized him. He was the guy who tried to get even for his friend. He also tried to knee me in the groin. In the past year he had put on an extra fifteen pounds of muscle. I said, "Just follow the rules, and no one gets hurt."

"Yeah, sure," he said.

I nodded toward the girl. "Does she know you're buying a win?"

"What she knows don't concern you," he said. "You just do what you're paid to do."

After Billy Bob left--I wouldn't say he walked out, more like strutted--the boss peeled off twenty dollars and passed it to me. "A bit more than usual," I said.

"He wants it to look extra good."

"He's an ass," I said. Before the boss could misconstrue my meaning, I held up my hand, waving the money. "I know. It's all about this. Don't worry. I'll do what's expected."

He looked over his shoulder at the departing couple, the guy's arm around the girl's waist, his hand low on her hip. "I guess he figures to get a little tonight if he wins. From her looks, I'd say she's worth it."

By the time the match rolled around, every seat was

taken and twenty or thirty people stood at the rear and along the sides. I figured Billy Bob had spread the word, and from the look of the crowd, they expected to see him victorious. I wasn't going to disappoint them. The guy paid his money, and I intended to give him and his friends what they wanted.

The ref turned out to be the big ranch hand I beat in my very first match. Still, since the fight was fixed, that didn't bother me. We met in the middle of the ring. The ref read the instructions from a card, we shook hands and returned to our corners. As I turned and faced Billy Bob, I saw his girl seated directly behind him, her expression blank as if she had little or no interest in what was about to happen. Either she knew because Billy Bob had told her or she figured it out on her own.

Even before the sound of the bell, whistles and catcalls sprang from the audience, encouraging Billy Bill to tear me apart. Just as before, he started slow, pushing me around with ease. Once he delivered a forearm uppercut that sent me back against the ropes. He followed that with a headlock, putting all his muscle behind the grip. Even that I didn't mind. He wanted to put on a good show. This I understood. Then his thumb twisted into my eye. I let out a yell and broke free. He came at me again, a smirk spread all over his face. He was enjoying himself.

I went into a clinch. "What the hell you doing?" I whispered

He kneed me in the groin. I never saw it coming, and he caught me square in the balls. It felt like he drove them right into my belly. I doubled over. He grabbed a handful of hair and clubbed me behind my head. I hit the canvas face down, the world spinning away.

When I came to, I was in my corner on a stool, the other two muscle-heads waving smelling sauce under my nose and splashing my face with cold water. "Did he pin me?" I asked. One of the guys shook his head. "He should have," I said.

In a world far away, I heard the bell for the second round. They pulled the stool out from under me, and I leaned against the turnbuckle for support. I must have looked like a wounded pigeon, and Billy Bob charged across the ring, intent on inflicting more punishment, but when he reached for me, I flicked my fingers into that hollow area just below his Adam's apple. I didn't put much force behind it. If I had, I could've killed him.

His eyes went wide, and he grabbed his throat, trying to catch his breath. I kicked his knee, hard enough that the kneecap snapped out of its socket. A thing like that hurts like hell, but the poor bastard couldn't find his breath to scream. His legs folded under him, and he sat down hard.

I caught a glimpse of his girl as she came to her feet, her eyes suddenly alive and interested.

The ref tried to give his friend a break and came between Billy Bob and me, pressing both palms against my chest to hold me back. "Get out of my goddamn way," I said. The tone in my voice frightened him, and he backed off.

I stepped behind Billy Bob and caught him in a sleeper hold. On TV I had seen wrestlers like Mr. Moto and Duke Keamuka apply sleepers, but that was all show. If you really know how to apply one, you can have a guy unconscious in fifteen seconds, brain dead in a minute and a half. Billy Bob didn't have much fight left in him, and he went right to sleep. I let him fall back and covered him. His friend counted very slowly, but he couldn't put off the inevitable.

I waited in the corner while his friends helped Billy Bob from the ring, so groggy they had to roll him under the bottom rope. His kneecap had slid back into place, but he would limp around for a few days. I thought trouble might come from his friends, and I was ready to take them all on if necessary, but none wanted a piece of me.

The Boss waited backstage. The moment he saw me, he said, "You were suppose to lose. Remember?"

I took a seat in front of a mirror and examined a cut under my chin where Billy Bob caught me with the uppercut and my swollen eye where he gouged me. My balls still hurt, my nausea so bad I thought I might throw up. I looked at the boss through the mirror. "The rube didn't play by the rules, and when a guy doesn't play by the rules, he doesn't deserve to win."

"So you took it on yourself to break the contract?"

"No sir. He broke the contract. I just informed him of that."

"And his money?"

I stood, and faced the boss. "I'd say he's forfeited it. That's what happens when people break contracts. I guess my only concern is that he might complain to the cops."

The boss smiled, which he seldom did. "If he did, everybody in this county would know he tried to bribe his way to a win. That would be worse than losing."

"Are you going to give him back his money?" I asked.

"Hell no. But next time, I'll make sure the rube knows he better play by the rules. The way that bastard dropped, I thought you killed him. Scared the crap out of me." He turned on his heels intending to leave, but when he tossed back the flap, the redhead was standing there. Up close I could see she was older than I first thought, maybe twenty or twenty-one, but she was prettier and softer looking, too, especially since she was smiling, and that smile was directed at me.

The boss looked back, his grin growing wider. "I guess sometimes it ain't about the money."

CHAPTER SIX

The Boy With Too Much Hair

We had just begun to set up on the edge of Los Baños for their Frontier Days. Usually the San Joaquin Valley in summer can be hotter than hell, but a heavier-than-usual ground haze filtered the sun so that it barely penetrated. I figured that by night we would be sitting in a heavy fog.

I found a pay phone at an Esso station just down the road and gave Osgood Warbling a collect call at his home in Fresno, which I did every week to update him on our take and expenses. "You heard Smith and Prescott folded," he said. "I bought one of their attractions. Let me tell you, it's going to put Warbling Brothers Road Show and Circus on the map. People are going to take notice of us now. We're moving into the big time."

I didn't ask what he bought. As a matter of pure fact, I said as little as possible to him. He had a temper that usually started with pissed off and quickly jumped to downright mean.

"When can I expect it?" I asked.

"They'll be there before night. Get it up and running by tomorrow."

Sure enough, around dusk a flatbed truck came rolling in carrying a tent and poles for a big attraction. A converted school bus lagged behind, the windows blacked out.

The truck rolled to a stop, and a tall, skinny blond climbed down from the passenger's side. She didn't wear any makeup, and I figured her for thirty or thereabouts. "We been on the road since six this morning, all the way from Ajo, Arizona. Need to stretch my legs." She stood half a head taller than me, but she was so thin that if she turned sideways, she might disappear. "Where do we set up, Boss?"

"West end. The ground's a little grassy, but there's plenty of room." I stepped to the truck and threw back a portion of the tent to reveal a couple of words, enough for me to understand. "Are you part of this?" I asked.

"I'm Ruby, the girl who can tie herself in knots."

"How many are you?"

"Besides me there's Anatol, the three legged Russian, and Vilma, the bearded lady, and Stacy the half man, half woman, and Leon the pin head." Then as an after thought, she said, "Oh, and there's Benji."

"Benji? Sounds like a dog act?"

"He's just a kid," she said, "but he's the hairiest kid you've ever seen--the hairiest person you've ever seen. He and his father joined us after Smith and Prescott sold the show, so they haven't signed on yet. We told them that was up to you."

"Ain't I the lucky bastard," I said. Frankly I never much cared for the kind of sideshow where the rubes gawked at the freaks. That old saying is true, you know, there but for the grace of God--

I shot a thumb toward the open field "Get moving. You need to be ready by morning. That's what Mr. Warbling wants, that's what he'll get."

"What about Benji and his father?"

"I'll follow you down and talk to them," I said.

By the time I caught up with them, I found the father slouching against the bus. The bus door stood open, and the occupants were already in the process of unloading the truck.

The father looked old and worn out and sick. His face was bloodless and full of wrinkles. Heavy bags hung under his eyes, and he was almost as thin as Ruby. When he saw me approaching, he perked up some and forced a smile, but he still looked like a man who should have been in a hospital bed. "I'm Kyle Pendergast. My son Benji—"

"Where is he? I want to see him." I looked I looked at the troupe unloading the truck but didn't see the kid Ruby described.

"He's in the bus. I put him in his cage."

"His cage?"

He looked at the ground and kicked up dust with the toe of his shoe. "I thought you might like to see him the way he's displayed."

"So show me."

I followed him into the bus. At first because of the dark interior, I had trouble seeing much. He led me to the rear where the seats had been removed to create space for luggage and props. At first all I could make out was the steel cage about five and a half feet high, and within its confines, a dark figure huddled in a corner.

"Benji," Pendergast said.

Benji stood. Like a good many teenage boys, he was dressed in a t-shirt and jeans, but he was no ordinary boy. Shorter than most--he probably stood no more than five-one or five-two--he was as Ruby warned, the hairiest person I had ever seen. His forehead and cheeks were covered in it. It fell over his ears and hid the backs of his hands. It even spilled over the top of his feet.

"What's your shtick, Pop?" I asked Pendergast.

"I've made up a whole story to tell people. He's a wolf boy, see, raised by wolves," said the old man. "Found by hunters in the wilds of Canada and brought back to civilization. Give him your wolf yell, Benji."

The kid threw back his head and howled. I swear it was the clearest and truest wolf howl I ever heard, and I doubted anyone could have told the kid's from a real one. I know I couldn't.

I had to admit the kid was good, and the story of a boy raised by wolves had worked since Kipling. The rubes would eat it up. "You're on," I said. "One rule: don't cause trouble, either with the roustabouts or the performers or the rubes. You follow that, we'll get along fine."

Pendergast appeared relieved, and he shook my hand so hard I thought he wanted to take my arm right off at the shoulder.

By eight that evening the heavy haze turned to fog, shutting out the moon and stars. The new crew worked through the night, setting up the tent. Despite the fog, the valley remained hot, and I had to keep the windows of my trailer open. The crew setting up the show kept me awake half the night, and I doubt I got more than four hours sleep. When first light crept through my window, I climbed out of bed grumpy as hell.

Even before breakfast, I went to take a look at the setup and found Ruby giving the front of the tent the once over. When she saw me, she said, "How's it look, Boss?"

I had to admit the bannerline—those long banners that promoted what was inside--looked impressive and promised a lot, usually more than these kinds of attractions delivered. But they would draw in the paying customers.

"I've got one rule, " I said to Ruby.

"Mr. Pendergast told us." She looked me straight in the eye, and I liked that about her. "We never cause any problems. None of us."

"That's what I like to hear," I said.

Usually when new acts joined, I tried to meet them right away, let each person know I was boss, but if they needed anything I was there to help. That morning I just couldn't bring myself to take a look, not before breakfast. As it turned out, I didn't make the show that day, but the rubes did.

Every hour on the half hour, I watched people exit the tent, their faces, white and drained, shaken by their encounter with some primordial force beyond their understanding. My God, that kid had it down pat, a call so wolf-like it made me want to rush right in there and throw open his cage and turn him loose.

So word got around, and people came from all over the county to see the Wolf Boy, the lines for each show often winding around the side of the tent. People stood in the hot sun sometimes close to an hour waiting to see him.

By early afternoon, the ground haze lifted. That night, the stars broke through the thin cloud cover, and the moon rose over the Sierra Nevada fifty miles to the east. At that point, the cries from Benji ceased, and people turned away from the show until only a few of the more curious purchased tickets for the next performance.

I went to see what the problem was. The show was going on when I entered, half a dozen rubes watching Ruby on the bare stage as she tied herself in knots. She wore a one piece stretch outfit that moved with her as she bent both legs behind her head and wrapped her arm around her legs. I found Pendergast back stage standing next to the cage, now completely encased in a thick burlap cover. "What's going on here? Where's the kid?" I asked.

"Benji's not feeling well." He wheezed when he spoke like he was out of breath. "I--I sent him to the bus. He's worn out. Night comes, the boy tires easily. Weak lungs. I'm sorry. It can't be helped."

"What is this?" I asked. "You trying to get yourself a bigger piece of the take? Is that it?"

Right then I thought I heard a movement behind the burlap cover, like a body shifting its weight.

"No, no, please. It's nothing like that," he said. "Benji and me are glad to be here."

"So what the hell's going on?"

"It's only his condition." With the back of his hand, he wiped his forehead, heavy with sweat. "He's a good boy, but his condition--"

"Why didn't you tell me this last night when you came in? For two cents--"

He looked fearful, like he thought I was going to fire him right then and there. "Yesterday we were on our last legs. If you hadn't hired us on, I don't know what we would've done."

Like most guys, I'm a sucker for a sad story, but in this business, you can't let sentiment influence your decisions. If I thought Pendergast and his boy would have been a drag, I would have sent them packing. But as much business as they drew in that day, I would have been a fool to let them go. "I'll cut you some slack," I said. "Just don't expect any more special favors."

Relief flooded his face, and his tense shoulders relaxed. "Thank you. Thank you."

Just then the burlap moved, a push outward like a hand brushed against it. Startled, I started to accuse Pendergast of trying to pull a fast one. His boy was still in there, hidden away by the burlap. Then a breeze touched my cheek, and looking over my shoulder, I saw people exiting through an open door. What the hell was I thinking? I asked myself.

I followed the rubes out to the midway. I guess I could've checked the other acts then, seen what else the show had to offer, but I could do that tomorrow. Or the next day.

As the night dragged on, I couldn't shake the idea that the boy was still locked in that cage. That's nuts, I told myself, yet I wandered the midway from one end to the other and back again, and I still couldn't shake the idea.

To put my suspicions to rest, I went to the bus to see for myself the boy was there. I pushed the door open and walked all the way to the back. Very little light from the midway penetrated, making the interior a black tunnel, but the kid wasn't there.

Their last show was at ten that evening, and I hid in the deep shadows under an oak. There I waited until the performers dragged themselves out the rear of the tent and boarded the bus. The three-legged Russian, came first, his third leg, a deformed piece of useless flesh, draped over one arm. The pin head followed, then the bearded lady, then the half-man-half woman, and finally, Ruby.

But where were Pendergast and his son? I waited another fifteen minutes, and still they didn't show. By then I knew they wouldn't. I left my hiding place and went to collect the night's receipts.

After I counted the take, the best Friday we ever had, I locked it away in the safe in my trailer, Afterward I pulled a bottle of Jack Daniels from the kitchen cabinet and poured myself a stiff drink. Thirty minutes later, I left the trailer and went back to the midway. It was well past midnight. We kept the lights on at the entrance and on the rides, but the tent lay at the far end of the midway. However, the full moon, now almost directly overhead, gave plenty of light, plus I brought my flashlight. I pulled back the tent flap and stepped inside.

Deep shadows closed about me. Almost immediately I sensed someone else in the tent. I flicked on the light, and a widening beam cut through the darkness. I walked back stage.

"I thought you'd come," a voice said. I shifted the light, and found Pendergast standing beside the cage, still covered by the burlap. "I hoped you wouldn't--I prayed to God you wouldn't--but I knew you would."

"I'm going to ask you once more," I said. "What's going on?"

A low growl came from the cage, and I shifted the light. I could see the silhouette of a body inside the steel bars.

"You bastard!" I said.

"You don't understand," Pendergast said.

I wanted to take the flashlight and pound his face in. How could a man treat his son like that? Show him during the day, make a wad of cash, but at night, hide him away in a steel cage, make him feel like a real monster.

I stepped forward, and I think Pendergast believed I was about to hit him. Maybe I was.

He reached over and pulled the cover away.

A violent roar filled the interior of the tent, and a body threw itself against the steel bars with such impact that for a moment the whole caged tilted and threatened to topple. The light caught the creature as it clung to the bars, the hands spouting claws, sharp and extended. It bared its teeth, except they weren't teeth but fangs, razor sharp, their ivory gleaming.

But it was its eyes that startled me, eyes surrounded by the dark fur, eyes that burned with hatred, eyes that said it wanted out of its cage to rip me apart.

The creature screamed, and I stumbled back, more scared than I've been in my whole life, before or since, and my elbow crashed into a supporting pole. The flashlight flew from my hand and hit the sawdust floor. Again the creature screamed, and I went down on my knees fumbling for the light as it rolled away. I grabbed it, and pointed the beam at the creature.

Pendergast threw the burlap back over the cage, and the scream died away. He turned and faced me, his expression one of sheer anguish. "I didn't want to show you. You gave me no choice."

"What is it?" My voice sounded hoarse and far away, like it wasn't me speaking.

"It's Benji. It's his condition."

My hand shook, and the light bounced from floor to ceiling, side to side. "Condition? My god, man, it wasn't human."

"Benji's human all right," Pendergast said, "It's just at night, he has these spells. He'll be fine in the morning. You'll see." I didn't respond right away. Frankly I didn't know what to say. Hell, I had never seen anything like this, and I suspected no one else had either. Right then I saw plenty of angles to this thing. Plenty.

My silence obviously worried Pendergast, and he said, "Look, Boss, you're our last hope. I mean, we got no money, and if you kick us out, we'll have nowhere to go. Even his mother doesn't want him."

"Does he stay in that cage all the time?" I asked.

"During the day he's fine. Like I said, it's only at night, and I sleep right next to him. I don't want anyone accidentally letting him out."

"Just how dangerous is he?"

Pendergast grimaced and shook his head. "I've never seen him hurt a soul--not one."

"He would have torn me apart, and you know it," I said.

"You frightened him. That's all." The old man was close to tears.

The cloth on the cage pushed outward, and a ragged claw broke through. I felt a surge of panic, fearful the creature intended to take a swipe at his father. Pendergast showed no such fear. The old man took the taloned hand in his, holding it as any father might hold the hand of his boy. Inside the cage the creature uttered a pathetic whine.

"Can we stay?" Pentergast pleaded with his eyes as well as his voice.

"Do the others know? The ones you came with?"

He nodded once, and I said, "As long as they know, I guess you can stay. Just make sure--"

"I never leave his side," he said. "Never."

I left the old man there with his son. I called him old, but maybe he wasn't so old. Maybe the strain of living and taking care of his boy had made him look old.

As for letting them stay--I didn't have to think on it. As long as Pendergast kept Benji in line, as long as the kid behaved himself, I'd keep them around. After all, in one day they proved to be the best box office I had seen in a long while, the best ever for Warbling Brothers. And if I could persuade Pendergast to show the kid at night, we would have one hell of an attraction, special shows that would knock the socks off the rubes. For those we could double the admission price--even triple it.

Hell, the kid was a goddamn goldmine.

# CHAPTER SEVEN

## Clowns

I was sitting across from Willie and Myrna Sanford, a husband-wife clown act, Fluggie and Flora, when Willie raised a fork and pointed to this kid standing off twenty-five or thirty yards, surrounded by dry brush and sand. He was watching the pie wagon. Or more specifically, he was watching the three of us as we ate.

He looked no older than fifteen or sixteen. He wore ragged clothes a size too large, probably hand-me-downs from an older brother, and the billed hat was pulled low over his forehead, hiding his brows.

Suddenly twin dust devils jumped to life on either side, swirling around the kid like angry ghosts. He swept the cap from his head, holding it tight to his chest to keep it from blowing away. The wind lifted his hair, long and black, and I realized he was a she.

For a moment she disappeared within moving brown walls. Then, as quickly as they appeared, the dust devils died, the sand hovering a moment in the air before settling back to the ground. The girl, covered in dust, so thick it blurred the definition of her face, slapped her cap back on her head, her long hair hanging loose over her shoulders.

"That poor girl," Myrna said. Like her husband, she was still dressed in her clown outfit, her face full of red and blue greasepaint. "You two go see she's all right."

Willie and I scooted back our chairs and trotted over to the girl. By then her vision had cleared, and she stared at us wide-eyed, like a deer confronted by mountain lions. I thought she was about to bolt. I wouldn't have blamed her if she had. I was still in my talker's outfit with my jacket, bow tie, and boots, and Willie was in his clown's makeup, a round, red nose, oversized red lips and a bright red wig. Perched on the wig was a top hat. His oversized shoes curved upward at the ends, so as he walked, his feet flopped in the dust.

Just as we reached her, the lid of his top hat flew open and out popped a clown in a pointed dunce cap, its face distorted with a malicious grin.

Up close, I still judged her to be no older than sixteen, maybe a year younger. She looked at us with big, dark eyes. Even though she wore loose, baggy clothing, her breasts pushed against her shirt, and through the material, I could the very faint outlines of areolas.

Despite the Boss promoting me to talker for the freak top, I was only twenty, and my experience with girls pretty limited. I could only stare at her. Willie broke the silence. "My sister sent us over to make sure you're all right."

"I'm hungry." She spoke with a slight Mexican accent. "I haven't ate in two days."

"What's your name?' Willie asked.

"Rosa," she said. "Rosa Vasquez."

"Well, Rosa, you better come on over. We'll see what we can do." Willie turned but Rosa held back as if afraid. Willie smiled, his clown's face lighting up. "Look, if I go back over to that table and you don't come, my wife will kill me. You don't want that, do you?"

Giving her my best spiel voice, I said "Come on over. See what we got." It sounded phony to me, and it must have sounded phony to her, too. My face burned with embarrassment, but she followed Willie and me.

Myrna came and took the girl by the shoulders and sat her down. By then, Myrna had already filled another plate with food and added a cup of java.

"I don't have any money." Rosa looked at me as if she expected I might throw her out. I guess my outfit made her think I had the power to do that, but I had only been with Warbling Brothers Road Show and Circus a year and a half, the Boss taking me on in late summer of '47. Willie and Myrna were old hands, so if they wanted to hand out a free meal, who was I to say different.

"You poor dear," Myrna said, one hand patting the girl's shoulder, the other creeping around her waist. "You must be starved. Go ahead now, eat your fill. There's more where that came from if you're still hungry."

Willie sat next to me, and I noticed he was staring at Rosa, too. Willie was in his mid-to late twenties, and out of his Fluggie costume, a handsome man, tall with blonde, wavy hair. His wife Myrna, whose costume differed from his only in the fact she wore no top hat, was his mirror image. A year or two younger and half a foot shorter, she was just as attractive as he was handsome.

"Is there anyone with you?" Myrna asked. The girl shook her head. "What about your family? They must be worried sick. Should we call your mother and father?"

With her fork, Rosa speared a piece of beef, the meat dangling like a dying fish. "I got no father. And my mother-- she got a boyfriend. She's had lots of boyfriends. The last one paid attention to me, so she kicked me out. Told me not to come back."

She concentrated on the food and finished the rest of the meal in silence. She stood up to go. "Thanks for the food," she said. "You're nice people.'

"Where are you going?" I asked.

She shrugged. "I'll find a place. I've learned how."

Myrna reached out and took the girl's hand. "Now, now, my dear. Let's not be hasty. You can spend the night here. Willie and I can make a place for you. Isn't that right, Willie."

"Absolutely." Willie nodded as he broke into a wide grin.

We were set up just outside Twenty Nine Palms, and other than the town itself, which was podunk hell, all that existed within twenty-five miles was desert. Myrna's offer was the best Rosa could hope for, and I certainly could broker no other option. Rosa said, "You'd do this for me? Why? You don't know me."

Myrna pulled on her arm, forcing Rosa back into the chair. "At one time or another, we're all poor travelers who need a bit of help from others. Willie and I have been in the same situation before. Isn't that right, Dear?"

"When we got our jobs here, we had twelve cents between us," he said.

Myrna patted Rosa's shoulder again, her arm once more

slipping around her waist. "Tonight you get a good night's sleep, and first thing in the morning, we'll see about a job. You'd like that, wouldn't you? Working here with us?"

"A job?" Rosa appeared confused. "I never had a job. I don't know nothing."

"It doesn't matter," Myrna said. "We can find something for you. Why, you're such a pretty girl. We'll get you cleaned up, and in the morning, show you to the Boss. Trust me, my dear, by this time tomorrow, you'll be comfortably settled in. Just leave it to me and Willie. We'll take care of you."

I think Rosa was unused to such kindness, and tears welled up in her eyes. She looked across at me. "I thought, the way you were dressed, maybe you were the boss."

"Me, the Boss? I don't even have the power to boss myself," I said. She laughed at my little joke, and I felt suddenly comfortable with her. "Look, I'll put in a good word with the Boss, too. Like Myrna said, we'll find you something."

"Absolutely," Willie said. His red nose wiggled from side to side, and the clown sticking out of his hat bobbled up and down.

Myrna laughed. "Oh, Willie, you do look a sight."

Sure enough the next morning Myrna took Rosa to meet the Boss. By then Rosa had bathed, and Myrna had given her one of her old dresses. They were close to the same size in height and weight.

"Can you dance?" the Boss asked her.

"Dance?" Rosa said. "I don't know nothing about dancing."

The Boss rubbed his chin, studying her. "You got a good figure and more than passable face. We could use another girl in the hoochie kooch, but if you can't dance--"

"Come on, Boss. None of the girls really dance," Myrna said. "They move their hips around, shake their behinds. Rosa can learn that easily enough. You're a smart girl, aren't you Rosa?"

"Smart enough, I guess."

So the Boss hired her.

The following week, I ran into Rosa at the pie wagon. By then we had moved on to Banning. She wore a harem outfit, all sheer muslin except for her bra and panties. She had piled her dark hair around her head, decorating it with bobbles and beads, and she looked like she stepped right out of an Arabian Nights movie. I asked her how things were going.

"Fine, I guess. I dance, men applaud." Her brow wrinkled, and she looked away.

"What's wrong?" I asked.

"I don't--" she began, then shook her head. She turned back to me. "People always want something from you, don't they?"

Myrna, dressed in her clown's outfit, sat her plate on the table and slid in beside Rosa. Right behind came Willie. "Hi there, honey." He laid his big paw on her hand.

Myrna took the girl's other hand and squeezed it.

Rosa looked across at me, her eyes empty like she had drifted off to another place. I left the three of them sitting there eating their food, and spent the rest of the day trying to forget what I saw. I kept telling myself I knew nothing, I only suspected. I was good at lying to myself.

On Saturday night, our biggest night of the weekend, the midway was packed. People stood in line for all the rides, and the concession booths did steady business reeling in the rubes. People filled the freak top for every performance. Even as I gave my spiel, I heard the music from the hoochie kooch, which was just across from us. After the ten o'clock show, I wandered out front, hoping to catch a glimpse of Rosa. I wanted to talk to her, but I had no idea what I wanted to say. Maybe I was worried about her.

Why I noticed the couple, I have no idea, except on this hot night, the man wore a jacket, his hand deep in his right pocket. The woman trailing kept pulling on his arm trying to hold him back. His dark face was twisted in anger as he stared up at the bannerline that showed half a dozen half-naked females surrounding a fat sultan who reached out for one of the girls.

The man in the jacket spoke in Spanish, then jerked free of the woman and headed for the rear of the top. Right then I understood it was trouble. I took off after them, rounding the top just as the two entered through the rear, his hand starting to come out of his pocket. I caught a glint of metal before the flap closed, shutting off my view.

As I threw back the canvas, they entered Rosa's dressing room, the man clutching one of those Army issued .45's that you could buy in any gun store.

I stopped just short of the dressing room where I could see everybody inside. Myrna and Willie in their clown outfits stood on either side of Rosa, the three of them facing the couple.

"What are you doing here?" Rosa asked.

"You come home now," the man said, his accent thick and guttural.

"I ain't going nowhere with you," Rosa said. "You can't make me."

The man raised the gun, his hand shaking. Myrna and Willie each took a step away back Rosa, their wide, painted smiles contrasting with the fear in their eyes. "You coming home or I'm going to kill somebody," the man said. He waved the gun first at Willie, then Myrna.

"Why--?" Myrna left the question unfinished as if she had forgotten the rest of what she wanted to say. Then sudden insight lighted her face. "He's your stepfather."

The woman spoke in Spanish, but the man ignored her. Rosa looked at her mother with disdain. "You wanted me gone, now I'm gone. I ain't going back. I'm staying right here with them."

The stepfather turned his angry gaze on Rosa's mother. "You kicked her out? You bitch, you dirty--" He cut off his words, too angry to finish. For a moment, the gun shifted toward the mother, but he caught himself and said to Rosa, "You come home now. She won't kick you out no more."

Rosa put her hands on her hips and glared at him. "I ain't going nowhere with you. I stay right here." She nodded toward Willie and Myrna. "With them I know what to expect. You--you're nothing but a stupid old drunk. Now go on. Get out of here. Or go to hell. I don't care."

At that point Willie summoned up enough courage to speak. "Look fellow, I don't know what you think is going on here--"

The stepfather swung the gun to cover Willie, and with his thumb, pulled back the hammer, the click loud even over the music coming from the front of the top. I was sure he was going to shoot Willie.

I looked around for a weapon, anything I could use, but there was nothing, not a spike, not a chair, not a piece of wood, nothing. The only thing I could do was rush in and tackle him from behind and hope the gun didn't go off and somebody get shot.

Rosa said, "Go ahead, shoot him. Shot me. Shoot us all. I don't care. Whatever happens is better than going with you."

I heard a loud sob, and I first thought it was the mother, but the gun wavered. "Please," the stepfather said, and he sounded very small and far away.

"You not going to shoot me, then get out," Rosa said. "Both of you get out. I never want to see you again. You both a piece of shit."

The mother reached across, and without resistance, pushed the gun down so that it pointed at the floor. In English she said, "I told you she wouldn't come back. You didn't believe me. You never believe me." She looked over to her daughter and spoke a word in Spanish.

"Same to you, Mama," Rosa said.

Grasping the arm of the stepfather, Rosa's mother led him out of the dressing room. Too lost in their own misery, they never saw me. The stepfather looked at the gun, surprised to find he still held it, and he dropped in his jacket pocket.

In the dressing room, Willie said, "My God, he was going to shoot me."

Myrna went to her husband and put her arms around him, holding him close. Willie began to shake like he had the chills.

Rosa laughed. "You were afraid, Willie? Poor boy."

"He could have killed us," Myrna said, her voice an octave higher than normal. "He could have killed us all. And the way you egged him on--it was like you wanted him to do it."

"So?" Rosa said. "What would have been so bad about that?"

At that point, I had enough. They didn't know I was there, so as quietly as possible, I turned and exited through the rear flap. By the time I reached the midway, the mother and stepfather had disappeared among the crowd.

I kept away from Rosa after that. Actually I kept my distance from all three. One afternoon Willie caught me at the pie wagon and asked why I was avoiding them. "You're just jealous," he said. "You were interested in Rosa, and you're just jealous."

I let him think that.

## CHAPTER EIGHT

## The Day the Sheriff Shot the Geek

Every geek I ever knew was a wino. He had to be to do what he did. Nobody else would take the job. We usually paid him off with a daily bottle of hooch.

Most didn't last more than a few months, seldom a year. With one exception, the geek I'm going to tell you about, this little guy Pookie Runyon, black as the blackest night and sporting this big grizzled beard streaked with gray. In those days before civil rights, he was the only black performer at Warbling Brothers Road Show and Circus, although we had half a dozen who worked as roustabouts.

He joined us in late spring of '47, and a year later he was still with us. Early on we could see this guy was a little better then other geeks. He never missed a performance, no matter how bad his hangover, and he was always changing his makeup, trying to look more authentic or at least more frightening. When he performed, he put a little extra into his screams, and he would jump up and down and flap his arms like a big monkey. He told me once, "That's the way the rubes see me. I ain't nothing but a big monkey to them. Shit, man, they can't see me any other way."

"Then why do it?" I asked.

"It's part of the act." He sat on the ground, his back propped against a tent pole. Tilting a bottle of Ripple, he took a long drink, his Adam's apple bobbing as he swallowed. When he set the bottle down, he said, "Hell, I may be nothing but a old drunk nigra, but my act is my act. It's what I do."

Our geek show was an annex to the Freak top. After the rubes paid their money and saw the pinhead, the wolf boy, the contortionist, the blade glommer, the three-legged man, our inside talker took over. That was me. I was pretty young in those days, but I had a strong voice, and when I gave my spiel, it carried well.

Once everyone had seen the other acts, I pointed to an area right of stage. "Behind this curtain, right there, not ten feet from where I stand, is the most spectacular, the most sensational sight you'll ever see. Ladies and gentlemen, we have spared no expense to bring you this most incredible, this most edifying attraction. You read about him in the papers, you've heard your friends and family talk about him, now see him for yourself-- the Wild Man of Borneo, brought to the shores of America for the first time. He lived with the animals, he lived like an animal, and you can see him in his natural habitat for just an addition twenty-five cents. Yes sir, one quarter brings you the most awesome, the most fearful sight you've ever set your eyes on."

At that point, Pookie lets out a cry so loud and piercing the rubes jump like scared cats. "Now, now folks," I would say. "Nothing to fear. He can't get to you. You're as safe as if you're in your own home. But right now it's feeding time, folks. He's impatient. Hurry now. Don't miss a minute of this. You'll remember it all your life."

Anxious to part with their two bits, the audience floods in. The rubes gather around a barred enclosure, the lights exposing only a few harmless snakes slithering around on the dirt floor along with a couple of chickens pecking for food. On the other side of the pit, a door flies open and in jumps Pookie dressed in a leopard outfit that covers his chest and loins. He crouches behind the bars of the cage and goes into his monkey dance, his eyes darting around the crowd until he spots a pretty girl. With a sudden yell he launches himself at her. Screaming, the girl jumps away from the cage. I bang my cane on the bars, driving him back. He begins to drool, and with a sudden swipe, Pookie seizes one the snakes and bites off his head. Blood sprays over him and the floor. Women scream, men shout, and the tent empties faster than air going out of a balloon.

It was a stupid act, and long ago the S.P.C.A. put a halt to the geek shows. Anyway, today's audiences are too sophisticated. Who would believe such nonsense?

But Pookie was good, the best I ever saw, and when he was sober and not suffering from a hangover, which wasn't very often, I enjoyed talking to him. Once he asked me, "Why you always hanging around, wanting to gab? Don't you have any white friends?"

"You tell great stories," I said. "I like hearing them. You're an interesting guy, Pookie."

He grunted a laugh. "My stories--hell, they ain't stories. They's my life. Why you think I's a drunk?"

"I meant no disrespect," I said.

He nodded, and with both hands scratched his full beard. He was always scratching his beard. "I guess a man's life is nothing more than a bunch of stories, 'cept they all just connect. Some stories better than others. Some lives better than others. Right now I's a geek in a sideshow. End of story."

"You're a good geek, the best I ever seen," I said.

"That's all I got." With that, he wandered off with a bottle tucked under his arm to drink away the afternoon.

On our final day in each city, usually a Sunday, around five in the afternoon as interest in the geek show sagged, we staged a big time ballyhoo. Dressed in his costume, Pookie would break out of the freak top and flee down the midway. Following him from the tent, I would yell, "He's escaped! The Wild man's escaped!"

"Look Out!"

"Run for Your Life!"

"Call the Police! Call the Police. The monster's escaped!"

A police offer appears, a service revolver in his hand. He fires twice in the air, the shots reverberating over the screams of the rubes. Finally four men subdue Pookie and carry him back into the freak top.

At that point, I step on the stage and begin my call. "Step right up, folks. Buy your tickets right here. See the wild man up close and safe." The wild man is fine, I tell them. The cop only fired the shots to scare him.

The rubes surge forward, once more eager to buy tickets.

Of course it was a put up job. The gun was loaded with blanks, the cries of terror came from me and other carnies. The policeman was usually a town cop eager for a little extra cash and a chance to play a role in the show.

In late June of '48 we rolled into Hemet and began to set

up the midway. In those days the town was so small that it didn't have its own police force and depended on the County sheriff's department. As a kid, I attended high school in Riverside, and an acquaintance of mine from those years, Spencer Grossman, had joined the sheriff's department. The Boss asked me to get in touch with him and see if he wanted the part on Saturday night. I gave him a call, and Friday evening he caught me between shows. He was decked out in his uniform, his sheriff's badge pinned to his khaki shirt, which was wrinkled and needed a pressing. I took him out to the pie wagon, and over a cup of java, explained the gig.

Spencer was a big blond kid who played football and had movie star looks. As I remember, he wanted to go into the movies, but he wasn't particularly bright. He told me he made a couple of screen tests, and one agent wanted to change his name to 'Stone' something-or-other. However, nothing came of it, and Spencer wound up staying in Riverside. I guess I was surprised he had enough smarts to make deputy sheriff.

I passed him a couple of blank shells for his .38. "You wait by the baseball concession. The geek comes running out, we shout and scare the hell out of everybody, then you step in. Fire a couple of shots in the air. Our guys jump the geek, cart him away."

"And for this, I get ten bucks."

"You understand what you're supposed to do?" I asked.

He grinned. "Easiest ten bucks I ever made." He slipped the blanks in his shirt pocket.

The next evening Pookie and I stood just inside the freak top waiting for him to stage his 'escape.' The smell of wine clung to him like sour perfume, and his breath stank of the stuff. His eyes were glassy but focused, and when he asked for a cigarette, his voice was steady. As much as he drank, I seldom saw him affected, although I was sure all that liquor dulled his senses enough to allow him to do his act.

I gave him a Chesterfield and a light. He puffed away until it was half gone. The Boss didn't like us to smoke in the tops--too much danger of a fire--but I always let Pookie have a puff before his 'escape.'.

"So a friend of yours is playing cop tonight," he said.

"He's not exactly a friend. I knew him in high school is all."

"Is he a good cop?"

I parted the tent flap and peered down the midway. Spencer, decked out in his uniform, stood just where I told him. "We played ball together. He was a lineman. Good but lazy. Didn't like to practice."

Pookie dropped the butt in the sawdust, crushing it under his heel. "If you got talent, you should give it everything you got. Ain't that right?"

"Right as can be," I said.

The time came, and Pookie had a surprise for me. From inside his leopard skin, he pulled a bottle of hydrogen peroxide. Opening it, he gargled and spit it out. He capped the bottle, threw it behind the bleachers and charged outside, giving off his Wild Man yell. By this time, he was foaming at the mouth.

I came on his heels. "He's escaped. He's escaped. The Wild Man's escaped!"

The crowd parted as Pookie darted right and left, his arms waving, the foam spreading back over his shoulder, and I could see the fear in the eyes of the rubes. They thought this was the real thing, a monster escaped from its confines, a rabid animal, and he was headed directly for Spencer.

But it wasn't only the rubes who were scared. From fifty feet away, I saw it in Spencer's eyes, too. He reached for his pistol. I started to yell to him, to remind him it was only an act, but I caught myself. There was no need. He was firing blanks.

The bark of the .38 was loud and clear even above the clatter of the rides and the shouts from the midway crowd. Blood spurted from Pookie's left arm, and without a sound he dropped. Spencer fired again, and dust flew up three feet to my right and whined off through the top. "What the hell!" I ran forward waving my hands. "Stop firing! Stop firing!"

Spencer stood clutching his weapon, his hand shaking. He stared down at Pookie who lay on his back holding his left arm, blood running between his fingers. I reached Pookie at the same time as three roustabouts. Together we lifted him and hurried to one of the dressing rooms. He didn't say a word until we settled him a chair. "That cracker friend of your done shot me," he said.

While we waited for the doctor, I went back to the midway to find Spencer. He still stood next to the baseball concession. He had holstered his pistol, and he wore a big smile like everything was all right. "What the hell happened?" I asked.

"Aw, I forgot to load the blanks."

"You could've killed him," I said. "Hell, you almost killed me."

He shrugged. "Nobody got hurt but the nigger. Anyway, he acted so real. I mean--I thought--."

"You stupid son-of-a-bitch!" I turned and walked away.

To my back he said, "Do I still get my ten dollars?"

Later after the doctor bandaged Pookie's arm--it turned out to be a flesh wound that removed a little skin and nothing more--I apologized for Spencer. Pookie was sitting up in bed, the white bandage around his arm contrasting with his dark skin. "Why'd the cracker shoot me?" he asked.

I laughed. "You scared the bejesus out of him. That hydrogen peroxide did the trick."

He broke into a smile. "He thought I was for real? Hey, man, that's all right then. I guess I was pretty convincing." He rubbed the outside of the bandage. "You thinks you can get me an extra bottle for today. This is starting to hurt pretty bad. I needs something to take off the edge."

The Boss sprang for a bottle of the good stuff--Jack Daniels as I recall--and Pookie got drunk very quickly. Despite the hooch and despite the wound, Pookie performed twice again that night, once at seven and again at nine, playing to packed houses. By then everyone wanted to see the Wild Man From Borneo who bit off the heads of snakes and chickens.

# CHAPTER NINE

# Hello, Dali

I'd been fiddling with the radio a good five minutes trying to get a clearer signal on the old Philco when I heard footsteps outside my trailer. For a moment, the static faded enough for me to hear a voice announce The Jack Benny Show, then it disappeared. Right after that, knuckles rapped on my door. Cursing under my breath, I flipped off the radio, disappointed I would miss Benny and Rodchester.

I took a couple of deep breaths before I answered. For the past five years I had run the Warbling Bros. Road Show and Circus for old man Warbling. In addition to being the Boss, I was also mother, father confessor and psychiatrist for the crew and performers. When they had problems too big to handle, they came to me. Mostly I just listened. Once in a while I was even able to help. I figured things ran more smoothly because I treated them like I cared.

So I opened the door with a smile, and there stood Dali. I don't think I ever knew his first name, and if I did, I've forgotten it. Everybody just called him Dali. When the guys would make a joke about his name, the kid took it good-naturedly. He took most things that way, which had to be a little hard for him. I would've expected him to be bitter, you see. In addition to a nose that spread all over his face and huge thick lips, he had a hump that rose out of his back that made him look like he was carrying around a boulder. All hunched over, I doubt he stood much over five feet. He had hired on in Fresno just over a year back, and in all that time, I never heard one of the guys say a mean word about him. And he was a good worker. Never complained more than the next guy. I put him in charge of all the rides, and he ran the baseball booth--you know, the one where the rubes throw balls at the wooden bottles.

"What's up, Kid?" I asked.

Ordinarily he wore a cap to cover his balding head, but now he clutched it in his hands, all wadded up. "Come to ask favor, Boss."

I ushered him in, but he didn't speak until I closed the door, like he didn't want anybody else to hear what he had to say. He looked up at me with sad eyes like those of a scolded puppy dog. "Today's my birthday. I'm twenty-one."

"You want tomorrow off? If that's the favor you're asking for, forget it. We're going to need everybody."

He shook his head, his thin hair whisking around his ears. "Nothing like that."

"Then what?"

His face turned red, and his gaze shifted to the floor. "I--I want you--to get me a present." At that point he found the guts to look me straight in the eye. "You don't have to buy it. I'll pay for it. You just have to find it."

"What the hell you talking about?"

"Like I said--I'm twenty-one today."

"Yeah, I heard."

"I'm twenty-one, and I've never been with a woman. I want a woman for my birthday." He had trouble getting the words out, like they was stuck in his throat. "I'm willing to pay. I got money. All I want you to do is find me one."

That kind of knocked me back on my heels. I didn't know what to say.

"I seen women come to your trailers," he said. "Most every town, you have a woman."

"So?"

"Do you ever pay for them?"

"Jesus, Kid. That's a damn personal thing to ask a guy," I said.

"Do you? Do you ever pay?"

That was the moment when I was about to kick him out. I mean, he had a lot of gall to ask me a question like that. But then I got to thinking--if I was twenty-one and never had a piece of tail, I'd be pretty desperate, too. I'd be willing to do just about anything if I thought it would get me laid. "Yeah, sometimes I pay," I said at last.

"So you can find me a woman."

"This is a podunk town. Ain't much here except desert and rattlesnakes. And besides, you're asking a lot." I looked into those eyes, and saw them water like he was going to cry. I hate it when I see a guy cry. It makes me despise him a little for being weak, and it's never good to feel like that toward a guy who works for you because he can make life miserable. He can sluff off on the job or give you plenty of lip, and pretty soon you got to fire him and hire another guy. In this business, good workers are hard to come by. Mostly you get bums and winos so desperate they'll take any job. So I said, "I don't like doing this. It feels like pimping, but if you're so set, we'll give it a try. Just don't expect much."

He grinned and reached in his back pocket, bringing out his wallet. He started to pull out a wad of bills. I shook my head. "You hold on to your money, Kid. Pay her when we get her."

We walked into Hemet, less than a quarter a mile from our encampment. It wasn't much in those days. A two-lane highway ran through the center of town, and it had a half dozen side streets. It was so small that it didn't even have a movie theater. But it did host Wild West Days, a weekend event that drew people from all over the county, which is why we came here in the first place.

Right off the highway, we found a bar called the Last Chance (How many times have I had drinks in a place called Last Chance. Seemed every little town in the West had a bar called that.) It was packed with men and women in cowboy hats and boots, and most everyone had a beer in his hand. A dozen or so stood around a couple pool tables in back watching amateurs knock balls around like they knew how to play the game. The place was full of amateurs.

I spotted the pro right off. She sat at the end of the bar nursing a Bud. Even from across the room, I could see she was past her prime and trying to hide it with too much makeup and a blonde wig that sat slightly off center, which made her appear like she listed to the left. She carried an extra twenty pounds, but she had a big set pushed up by one of those pointed bras.

I had left Dali outside, figuring I could work a better deal alone. The pro saw me eying her, and she sat up a little straighter, lifting her bottle and waving me over. I sat on the empty stool next to her.

I flagged down the bartender and ordered a beer. He opened a bottle and set on the bar, waiting while I dug out four bits. I took a good long swig of the cold brew before I swiveled to face her. She wore a low cut dress and leaned heavily on the counter, showing a lot of cleavage. It took your eyes off her face.

She smiled. "You looking for a date, Honey?"

"I got a friend outside who is."

She narrowed her eyes in suspicion. "Why doesn't he come in hisself?"

"He's bashful. This is his first time."

"How old is he? Twelve?"

"Twenty-one. Today's his birthday."

"He's twenty-one and still got his cherry. Now that's a downright shame." She flashed a crooked smile. "Well, I'll be glad to relieve him of that burden."

We haggled over price until we settled on $20 as long as it was straight sex. "And it don't matter how long he lasts," she said. "He gets his rocks off while we're getting undressed, he still pays up."

I led her outside. We stood under the neon light flashing "Last Chance," except the capital 'C' was missing. At first I didn't see Dali, and the pro said, "Well? Where is he?"

I spotted him near the corner of the building hiding in the shadows. "Come on over, Kid."

As he stepped into the light, the pro took a good, long look. I saw a momentary flicker of disgust cross her face, and I thought she might queer the deal then and there, but she wanted the money too badly. She reached out and took the kid's hand. "Come on, Honey. You come with Mama. I'm going to show you a real good time. I got a room just a couple of blocks from here."

The kid threw me a mournful look as if to say "What the hell do I do now?" I guess he was a little scared. I would've been if I was him.

She guided him off into the dark. After that, I went back inside. By the time I made it back to my trailer, I was lightheaded from half a dozen beers. Dali was waiting for me, sitting on the steps, his knees drawn up to his chest. When he saw me, he climbed to his feet. "So how did it go, Kid?" I said.

I fumbled with my key trying to push it in the lock. When I finally opened the door and stepped inside, Dali was right behind. He had a funny look on his face like he just flunked an exam and was afraid to tell me. "It didn't go well, huh?" I said.

He ran a hand through his thinning hair. "I get hard-ons. Every night I get them. They're so hard they hurt. I have wet dreams. I jack off."

"You couldn't get it up," I said.

"Who could with her? My god, she was older than God. Her wig slipped off, and all her hair underneath was gray. Screwing her would've been like screwing my grandmother."

"So what happened?"

"I gave her thirty just like you and her agreed, then I got the hell out of there."

"Thirty, huh?" I laughed.

He stared at me with those big puppy dog eyes, all watery. "It's my birthday, and I still didn't get my present."

I looked at my watch and tapped the crystal. "It's half past midnight. Your birthday's over, Kid."

"But--" He held out his hands palms up as if in supplication. "--but you promised."

This conversation along with all the beer was giving me a headache, and as always happens when I've had too much to drink, my temper was getting short. "I never promised a thing. Look, this isn't San Francisco or LA. There's not a lot of choice here. You take what you can get."

"Maybe we could drive over to Riverside or San Berdoo—"

I waved a hand, cutting him off. "It's already tomorrow. We open in a few hours. I need sleep and so do you. We got no time to go traipsing off."

His chin dropped on his chest, and he gave a loud groan. He wasn't exactly crying, but he was close. I couldn't let that happened. I softened and said, "Look--maybe we can try later down the road. There'll be other towns, bigger towns."

He lifted his head. "You mean that, Boss?"

"I ain't promising nothing, but we'll see." I pointed to the door. "Now go on, get out of here. Let me get to bed."

He shuffled out, not bothering to look at me. Maybe he

believed me, maybe not, but at that moment, I didn't a give a damn. I just wanted to get some shuteye.

Funny thing. I never mentioned it to him again, and even though he worked the circuit with us for another couple of years, he never said anything to me either. I figured he got one of the other guys to help him out. Or maybe he worked up enough courage to do it on his own. I hope so. I hate to think of a nice kid like Dali never getting a piece of tail, but really, what business was it of mine? I mean, the guy was asking a lot. Maybe too much. Right?

CHAPTER TEN

Possum Belly Queen

I crawled under a semi and opened the possum belly, a specially built compartment that held tent stakes and other equipment. I began tossing out stakes to a couple of the roustabouts. My main job was the caller--the barker--for the freak top, but like everyone else, I worked half a dozen jobs. We all shared the work.

The possum belly was a large container with enough room for a couple of people to squeeze in, and when I first joined Warbling Brothers Road Show and Circus, I slept in one when the Boss had nowhere else to put me. Actually they weren't too bad if you laid down a soft mattress first. They were cozy and warm, which proved good when we worked the desert towns during the summer and the nights turned cool. On warm nights, they held the heat so that you felt like you were sleeping in a steam room.

Of course, they were good for other things, too. When a town girl fell in love with a one the guys and acted accordingly, that was where he took her. We called such girls 'Possum Belly Queens.' Lots of guys bragged about the girls they shagged in one of those holes, but all I knew were the stories. I didn't have one experience like that--not one.

Now at the time I'm telling you about, early July '48, I was only twenty and beginning my second full season with Warbling Brothers. Earlier that year when Warbling Brothers acquired the freak top, the Boss asked me if I would like to be the caller for the show. I had a deep bass that carried well with or without a microphone. "And you got a mug that makes you look as innocent as a Catholic choirboy," he said. "Whatever you tell the rubes, they'll believe it."

I grew up in Riverside, California, never traveling

much beyond Los Angeles. In high school I made the varsity football team and started at halfback for two years. I was a jock, and I didn't lack for dates. But what the hell did I really know about girls? Not much. I dated, I groped a little, and a couple of girls let me undo her bras and feel her breasts. After high school I took a job at a gravel pit, not because I wanted to--I wanted to go to college--but my mother could barely afford to keep my little sister and me in food and clothes. I hated the gravel pit, six twelve-hours days of back-breaking work. So Warbling Bros. came to town, and when it left, I left with it. I wasn't making any more money than before, but I had a place to sleep and three squares a day. On top of that, I got to travel. The job wasn't the romantic adventure people often believed, but it was a hell of a lot better than the gravel pit.

Now I've spent a lot of time explaining things to you, but you need to understand before I tell you what happened next.

For the past hour, we watched dark clouds roll in from the east. The one thing that could disrupt an organization like ours was a storm, and like most of the guys, I kept my eye on it. That's how I spotted the girl, a couple of books tucked under one arm, coming up a dirt footpath fifty yards to the south. Her hair caught my eye first, a splash of red lifted by the breeze and flaring back over her shoulders. With each step her hips swayed and her skirt moved with them, the two in a silent dance. I figured she was sixteen, maybe seventeen, on her way to school.

I came out from under the truck, shading my eyes to see more clearly. She glanced my way, and for a brief moment, slowed. I raised my hand and waved, hoping for a response but not expecting one. Her eyes locked on me for a couple of seconds, but other than that, she made no gesture or acknowledgment.

A sudden gust of wind lifted her skirt well above her knee, showing me a shapely thigh. Hurriedly she pushed it back down, but not before my mind conjured up all sorts of pictures of what lay under that skirt.

"Wake up," one of the roustabouts said, "We could use a little help here."

So she walked on, and I went back to work, figuring I would never see her again.

The storm held off, and just past seven that night, everything was up and ready to run, and the Boss gave us the rest of the night off. I cleaned up and went into to town, a vague hope floating around the back of my mind that I might see her. Today when you drive the freeway, Azuza with its undefined, nebulous boundaries seems an extension of LA, but in those days, it was a truck stop along Route 66. I got a hamburger at a greasy spoon, and afterward, walked the darkening main street, the movie theater the only business still open. The marquee announced a double feature, THE KISSING BANDIT paired with DARING CABALLERO. The one sheets behind the glass showed the first a romantic comedy, the other a western, and the sign at the ticket booth said I could see both for only fifteen cents, a Thursday night special. How could I resist such an offer?

The lobby smelled of mildew. I bypassed the concession counter and went right into the theater, sliding into an aisle seat, the cushion lumpy, the torn fabric repaired with electrical tape. The western was more than half over, and I endured the Cisco Kid for another twenty minutes before it mercifully ended followed by previews of coming attractions. Afterward I sat through ninety minutes of Frank Sinatra flitting between Kathryn Grayson and Ann Miller. I left the movie theater disappointed, the advertisements out front having promised far more than they delivered.

The next day we opened just past one, and by four, the midway began to fill, lines forming for the Ferris Wheel and the Hammer. The storm clouds from the day before had returned, hovering just over the mountains to the north, and as long as they stayed there, they presented no problems, but an hour later, they had moved closer, thunder announcing their eminent arrival. The tents flapped in the wind, and dust swirled down the midway. Despite these conditions, I went out front to begin my spiel, and soon a small crowd formed.

I spotted her standing near the front, a book tucked under one arm, the wind lifting her red hair around her head. Up close I could see she was damned cute, her face full of freckles, her sweater hugging her round, full breasts. Right then, I began playing only to her. She didn't smile, she didn't frown, she just stared at me. I upped my volume, I waved my cane at the bannerline, I hopped around the stage, and still no reaction, just that steady, unwavering gaze.

After ten or fifteen minutes, Marion who sold tickets gave me the high sign that the place was nearly full, and I went inside to introduce the acts--the three-legged man, the wolf boy, the contortionist, the pinhead, the sword swallower, the fire eater, the half man-half woman, the alligator man, and finally, if the rubes paid an extra two bits, the Wild Man From Borneo. The place was packed with more than a hundred bodies.

No sooner did I step on the indoor stage than she came through the tent flap and stood near the rear, partially hidden behind two burley guys in overalls. So what? I thought. She's just a curious rube like all the other rubes. So I paid her no more mind and went about introducing the acts to the ooohhhs and aaaahhhhs of the audience. Finally I delivered the come-on for the Wild Man of Borneo--our geek show--and while Marion collected addition two bits from thirty-five or so customers, I searched for the girl, but she was gone.

I told myself I needed a smoke, and since we never smoked inside the tops--too much chance of fire--I went out front where I looked up and down the midway. She was nowhere in sight. The thunderclouds had drawn closer, and lightning flashed followed by the rumble of thunder.

Disappointed, I lit up and wandered to the rear of the top, consoling myself with the Chesterfield, but after half a dozen drags, I stopped tasting it, tossed it in the dirt and ground it out with my heel. Things never worked out the way I wanted.

Behind me a voice, filled with mint juleps and magnolias, said, "You all have a real excitin' show, Mister."

I turned, and there she stood, the book still clutched under one arm, the rising breeze tossing her red hair around her head.

And then--

"I waited for you." I held out my hand.

She came to me. I swept her in my arms and kissed her full on the mouth. She dropped the book, her arms coming around my neck, her body pressed against mine so that I felt every curve and indentation of her body. She held me like she didn't want to ever let go, and I crushed her, so hard I felt her hot breath all the way down my throat.

But—
--that wasn't exactly the way it happened.
In reality, I stood speechless, not quite knowing what to say. She stared at me with big green eyes as if she expected something, and I didn't have a clue what it was. With a slight roll of her shoulders that I took for a shrug, she started to walk away. At that point I found my voice. "What--what are you reading?" I asked.
Right away I thought, Now that's a stupid question, but she didn't laugh at me. Instead she held out the book. Enough light from the midway penetrated the shadows so that I could read the title: FOREVER AMBER. "Have you read it?" she asked.
"I heard about it. I guess just about everybody's heard about it."
"It's my favorite book I ever read."
Lightning broke through the clouds, bathing the landscape in florescent white, and thunder exploded right on top of us. The girl and I both jumped, scared out of our wits. Right behind the thunder came the rain, not a sprinkle or a few drops, but a downpour, more like the height of a storm than the beginning, blinding in its ferocity.
'Come on!" I shouted, and ducked under the nearest semi. I didn't have to tell her a second time. She jumped in beside me. On the midway I heard people screaming and running for cover. The wind picked up, the freak tent snapping like an angry alligator, and rain swirled under the truck. Behind us a possum hole beckoned, and I touched the girl's hand, drawing her attention to it. The rain pounding the truck made it impossible to be heard, but she caught my meaning, and I helped her in and climbed in beside her. One of the roustabouts, planning to sleep there, had laid a mattress down, and we faced outward. Within minutes, a good inch of water covered the ground beneath the truck.
We clung to each other, partly because of the confines of the possum belly, partly because of the chill from our damp clothes. I wasn't afraid. In fact, the whole episode was proving exciting, the two of us alone, lying on a mattress hidden from the world. Again lighting flashed and thunder exploded, and suddenly all the lights on the midway died, leaving us in almost

total darkness. She began to shiver, and I slid my arm over her shoulders. She moved into me. She must have felt my arousal, but she didn't shy away. Instead she held me even tighter.

The storm continued for a good ten minutes before the wind faded and the rain let up. By then I could hear water flowing like a river under the truck.

She looked up. "It's so dark."

"Nothing to be afraid of." I held her tight, not wanting to let go. "We're safe here."

"I've got to get home. My mama--"

"She'll understand."

"No," she said, the word sounding more like a plea than a denial.

On the midway, one of the roustabouts must have hooked up a generator because a rack of lights came to life. Her face was within inches of mine, her mouth so close that I could taste her breath, slightly sour like she had an upset stomach. It didn't matter. I wanted to kiss her, but I didn't. Maybe she expected me to. Maybe I disappointed her.

"I have to go home." She scrambled out of the possum belly. I tried to help her, but she pushed my hands away and half fell, catching the edge of the metal frame for support.

"Will you come back tomorrow?" I asked.

"No--I don't know. Maybe. " On her hands and knees, she crawled out from under the truck, and I heard her feet splash in the water as she ran away.

I started to climb out, too, when my hand touched her book, and I realized she had left it behind. "Hey, wait," I yelled, but she was gone. I took the book to my trailer and laid it on a table, figuring I could return it the next day. Afterward, I joined the crew, and we spent the whole night digging tents and booths out from mud.

The next morning, a Saturday, we were all dog-tired, but we opened on time to clear, bright skies. I waited for the girl all day and well into the night, but she never showed. I was still looking for her when we broke camp and pulled out of town.

A year later we returned to Azuza, and though I searched the crowds for her, I never saw her. I don't think I really expected to, but letting go of my romantic illusions proved more difficult than I would have expected. To this day I still have that copy of FOREVER AMBER, and whenever I come across it, I get a good laugh at my expense. Yet, at the same time, I cannot help but have a fond remembrance for my possum belly queen and what might have been.

## CHAPTER ELEVEN

## Miss Victoria

### 1.

Miss Victoria died on a Sunday while we were tearing down the midway. Only when people broke for dinner and found the pie wagon locked, the kitchen staff gathered outside, puzzled expressions on their faces, did we begin to suspect the worst. One of us ran to get the Boss. He came, and after repeatedly knocking on the door and calling her name, he took out his keys and let himself in her trailer.

He found her in the front living space, separated from her bed by a thick curtain. She was sitting in her one chair, the reading lamp still on, and in her lap, an open Bible. The Boss followed her finger to Psalms 61: "Here My cry, O God; attend unto my prayer. From the end of the earth will I cry unto Thee, when my heart is overwhelmed."

Miss Victoria sat with her head bowed like she was in prayer, her gray hair hanging loose over her shoulders, one wrinkled and flaccid hand palm up beside the Book. The Boss took the hand in his and felt for a pulse but found none. Stepping back outside, he locked the door, and turning to us, announced that Miss Victoria had passed on.

Others oversaw our meals that night, and we ate what was laid before us. Out of respect, we talked in hushed whispers, shocked and dismayed at our loss. For more than twenty years, Miss Victoria had been an institution, a revered soul on whom we depended for so much more than just food. Others might disappoint us, might lie to us, forget us, betray us, but we could depend on Miss Victoria, who cared for us far beyond our due. Not only was she our chief cook, she was our savior of souls, our mother confessor for those who believed in a higher power and for those who didn't. We could tell her our doubts, our fears, our most cruel secrets, and be assured they were safe with her, and in her, we found absolution.

If she had relatives, she never spoke of them, so she was ours and ours alone. We would brook no outside sources taking her from us. No one called the police or a funeral home. Later that night, after most of us dragged ourselves off to bed, the Boss moved Miss Victoria into the pie wagon and laid her among blocks of ice where she would keep.

The next morning the whole show left Indio for Julian where we would set up for the next weekend. Near Palm Springs, the Boss detoured our caravan off a road that ran through a desert canyon. We parked the heavy vehicles at a wide turnout, and most of us, fifty or more, crowded in pickups and cars and continued on a dirt road until we came to an old mining community of crumbled cabins and holes dug in the mountainside. We piled out of the vehicles and followed the Boss up the hill. He cradled Miss Victoria in his arms, her stiff, shriveled body small under a wool blanket. Hidden behind a ruined barn lay a graveyard, a dozen crosses marking the burial sites of those long dead.

A couple of us brought shovels, and we began to dig in the hard earth. Our carpenter collected a piece of ancient wood, large like a plaque one might hang on a wall. With a chisel and hammer, he carved delicate words:

Miss Victoria
Who cared for us all
In Loving Memory

Afterward he rubbed sand into the words to make them appear as old as the town itself. We didn't want anyone stumbling on a fresh grave and digging her up.

We laid her in the hole, careful not to break her tiny frame, still frozen from her night in the ice room. Quickly we covered her with dirt and rocks, and smoothed out the top with tumbleweeds and brush so it appeared no different from the other graves. Only then did the Boss read a scripture form the Bible, "Yea, though I walk through the Valley of the Shadow of Death," he began, "I will fear no evil."

And so, we laid Miss Victoria to rest and returned to our

work because we were not the ones dead.

Yet we all felt a hole in our lives, as if a part of us had gone missing.

2.

We sat around the pie wagon eating supper, when one of us asked the Boss how he first met Miss Victoria. He laid aside his knife and fork and wiped his mouth with his napkin. "It was September of '34, and I was ignorant kid from Dallas. My mother had three more of us, and because I was the oldest, she kicked me out. I don't blame her. As I see it, she didn't have much choice. I didn't see it like that then, but what the hell? I survived. I rode the rails, a bum living in hobo camps, begging for meals, stealing them when I had to. With winter coming on, I headed for California. It was in Thermal where three yard bulls caught me and this other guy, Joe, and threw us off the train."

The bulls laid a couple of ax handles across their backs and sides before they tossed the Boss and Joe off the train just as it was gathering speed, the ground a passing blur. The Boss slammed into the hard packed desert floor and was out for twenty or thirty minutes. When his senses finally cleared, he tried to sit up. Pain ripped through his right side with such fierceness it took his breath away. The bulls had busted a couple of ribs, but when he glanced at his traveling companion, he realized he had gotten off lucky. Joe, a kid no older than the Boss, lay very still, his neck twisted at an unnaturally oblique angle.

Holding his elbow into his side, the Boss tried to get to his feet. He made it on the fifth try. Standing on unsteady legs, breathing through his open mouth, he could see two tents, a Ferris Wheel and half a dozen large trucks less than three hundred yards to the north. It was already past four, the sun dropping toward the western mountains, and people had begun to wander the midway.

He managed to stumble almost the entire distance, but twenty feet from the pie wagon, he dropped to his knees, and when he tried to get back to his feet, he passed out. When he came to, he was in a bed with starched sheets, a pillow under his head, his dirty clothes gone, his chest and ribs enclosed in a tight bandage. Miss Victoria stood over him with a glass of water. "Don't worry, my boy." She lifted his head and tilted the glass to his lips. "You're in my hands now, and I'll take good care of you."

Later he learned that when they found him, old man Warbling wanted nothing to do with him. "He's a bum. Let him be."

Miss Victoria stuck a thin, arthritic finger in his face. "That's not what we'll do. He's only a poor boy who needs a helping hand."

The old man chewed tobacco, and he spit, a brown glob rolling in the dust. "He'll rob you blind if you let him."

"He's mine, and that's that." With her hands on her hips, she glared at him, and he knew better than to offer any more objections.

3.

Miss Victoria came to us long before most of us even knew of the existence of Warbling Brothers Road Show and Circus. That was in the mid '20s while the county was still flying high from the end of the First World War and before the Great Depression came along and sent everything spinning out of control. The show was smaller then, a couple of rides and the big top.

She showed up one day hauling an old steamer trunk, one on wheels so that it bounced along the ground. The trunk bore no stickers of far away exotic lands, no evidence of travels except dents and scratches, and the brown paint had long ago weathered away until all that remained was bare wood burned black by the sun.

The show was in winter quarters in Richmond, right across the Bay from San Quinten. In those days the prison had a separate section for women, so it was only natural when Mr. Warbling saw Miss Victoria for the first time, lugging that beaten up steamer trunk, her clothes old and ragged, he figured her for a just-released inmate. Not trusting convicted felons, he confronted her with the intent of demanding she leave, but she shook her head. "No sir, you've got it all wrong. I came to visit a relative. He got a cancer and died. Now I got no money and need a job. I'm real strong and can do most things a man can do, but you'd be better served if you let me cook for you."

Even then she had iron-gray hair and must have been pushing fifty. Mr. Warbling wanted to harden his heart against her, but her eyes, haunted eyes, reminded him of his own grandmother, dead so long ago, and he hired her, although adding a stipulation that if she couldn't cook, she would be gone the next day. He took her back and introduced her to Crusty Jones, a bewhiskered old codger in charge of the pie wagon. Well into his eighties, Crusty had worked chuck wagons for Texas trail herds. He could boil beef and potatoes, but beyond that, knew little of the culinary arts. Within a week, Miss Victoria ran the pie wagon, regulating Crusty to assistant, but he didn't mind. "Hell, now you peckerbellies can stop complaining about my cooking," he said. "I don't have nothing more to do with it."

Right after that, old man Warbling gave Miss Victoria her own trailer attached to the pie wagon. He even hauled her trunk in and offered to help her unpack. "It's just a few clothes and a keepsake or two," she said. "You go on now. I'll be fine."

Later when he returned, she had laid out clothes and blankets on the bed and a photograph on the dresser. "Not much for such a big trunk," Mr. Warbling said.

"Memories take up most of the space." She smiled, her hand resting on the top of the photograph where a young boy, no more than three or four, looked out unsmiling, his hair neatly combed, his clothes cleaned and pressed. When she saw Mr. Warbling staring at it, she said, "My little boy, my sweet little boy."

"Where is he now?"

Those haunted eyes watered, and she touched her breast. "He's here, with me."

As was his nature, Mr. Warbling asked no more questions, already knowing more than he wanted. "Yes ma'am, and good night to you." He hurried back to his own trailer and buried himself in the budget figures for the coming year.

## 4.

And so, Miss Victoria became part of the show, and in doing so, worked her way into our lives, although it was the men, especially the young men, with whom she showed such affection. Don't get me wrong and think that some sexual perversion motivated her actions. In these days of cynicism and opportunism, we find it easy to jump to such conclusions. But her heart was pure, and we harbored no suspicions.

Now I can tell you all sorts of reasons why we loved her so, but here I think it best to relate this one instance that happened only a few weeks before she died. Perhaps, in addition to showing Miss Victoria's humanity, the story tells something about ourselves, our callous attitude of taking her for granted. We should have seen she was ill, growing thinner, her face skeletal, her flesh so thin it appeared translucent. Yet, her eyes, haunted still, seemed so alert, so accepting. That is the only excuse I can offer for our failure to notice those ominous signs.

We had this kid named Nick, a 'forty-miler' we all thought, an expression we reserved for those we believed wouldn't stick with us forty miles down the road. He was seventeen or eighteen, and so soft that the first day of pounding the stakes, his hands blistered so badly they bled. Miss Victoria, who also served as our nurse, covered the wounds in salve and bandages. Afterward she slipped him a dollar bill. "There's a hardware store down the street. Go buy yourself some work gloves. You've got to protect those hands. They're the only ones you'll ever have."

That in itself was a generous act, but the very next day, a Western Union delivered a telegram. When the messenger found Nick, wearing his brand new gloves, he laid the hammer aside, his expression a question mark. He didn't bother taking off his gloves but ripped the envelope open with his teeth. He read slowly, his face screwing up like he was about to cry. "My mama," he said.

He asked the Boss for an advance on his salary, just enough to get him to LA, but the Boss was a businessman. "I don't pay for work until it's done," he said.

So Miss Victoria gave the boy another ten dollars, this time for a ticket back to LA, plus a little extra for food and whatever else he might need. "I'll pay you back. You can bet on that," the boy assured her.

When he had taken the money and gone, the Boss said to her, "You'll never see that money or him again, Miss Victoria."

She patted the Boss on the arm. "You think that matters. The only thing that matters is that my boy is happy tonight."

So she vanquished the Boss' objections over Nick just as twenty years before she vanquished the objections of old man Warbling over the Boss. The Boss knew better than to argue with her, too, and shaking his head in defeat, took himself off to see if the big top was up and secure.

We didn't see Nick again until after we laid Miss Victoria to rest in that graveyard in the old ghost town. We rolled into Indio and found him waiting out front of Thomas' Drugs and Emporium where the Greyhound Bus had let him off earlier that day. He waved to us as the caravan rolled down the one main street. When the Boss pulled his truck over to the curb, the kid slid in, smiling like he was glad to be back. "And I got money to pay back Miss Victoria," he said.

5.

The Boss waited the weekend before cleaning out her trailer because, he told himself, he was too busy setting up for the weekend, and then once the midway and rides were up and running, he had to see they stayed that way. It wasn't until the following Sunday night he forced himself to the task.

He took a barrel with the intention of throwing away trash that most people accumulated, but Miss Victoria had kept a well-cleaned abode, a dresser and table free of knick-knacks, her only accouterments a brush and a couple of combs, and the photograph of her son. Her clothes were neatly stacked in drawers, and from the closet, he dragged out the steamer truck, so old and worn, the leather from the handle flaked off in his hands. When he threw back the lid, acrid dust rose from the interior and burned his nostrils. Reaching into the dark interior, his hand came in contact with a scrapbook, which he lifted out, some of the ancient black coating sticking to his fingertips. One at a time, he brushed his hands on his pants before opening the book.

Except for the first five pagers, all was blank. On those five pages, Miss Victoria--at least he supposed it was her--had cut out and pasted a series of newspaper articles from *The Ventura Star Telegram*. Seating himself in the same chair in which he had discovered her body, the Boss began to read the clippings, all dated between July and December 1899. Combined, they told the following story:

On a very warm July 4th, a young boy of three, Willis Boggins McPherson, died after sustaining injuries when his frail little body fell under the wheels of a speeding carriage driven by a drunken Edgbert Fearly, the son of a socially prominent state senator. The young boy was survived by his parents, Jonathan and Victoria McPherson, who owned a local mortuary. After a closed casket memorial service, the couple laid their son to rest in a private cemetery of their choosing.

The police charged Edgbert Fearly with involuntary manslaughter. The trial lasted two days, at the end of which the judge, citing misconduct on the part of the prosecution, threw out the jury's verdict of guilty and dismissed all charges against the defendant. Less than two hours after the judge's decision, Jonathan McPherson boldly walked into the living room of the Fearly's residence and shot Edgbert Fearly six times while the latter celebrated his victory with family and friends. All told, more than fifty people witnessed the killing. The same judge who released Edgbert Fearly, sentenced Jonathan McPherson to life in prison without parole, calling the crime 'that of an unrepentant killer.'

By the time he finished the newspaper articles, the Boss had fallen into a state of depression. All the time he had known Miss Victoria, he knew nothing of this. No one had, and he wondered how she could have kept such misery bottled up without exploding. By god, what fortitude, he thought.

Rising from the chair, he dropped the scrapbook back in the trunk. He would take this out and destroy it so that no one else would see what he had seen, read what he had read. He would honor Miss Victoria's privacy. He would honor her secrets.

He had only one thing left to do--strip the bed and clean

up whatever else lay behind the gray, dusty curtain. He reached out, grabbed a handful of cloth and pulled it back, hearing threads rip, dust swirling in the air.

For a long time, he stared at the bed and the little boy who lay in it, a fine coating of dust clinging to dried, wrinkled flesh. Judging from his size, the boy couldn't have been any older than three or four, the features long ago turning brown, mummified, so that the face and hands appeared made of tanned leather. His arms were propped up so they simulated an embrace, and when the Boss bent over the body to examine it more closely, he saw, locked between bony fingers, strands of gray hair, and heard, almost as if she were in the room with him, Miss Victoria's voice: "My little boy, my sweet little boy."

The next morning before the sun rose, the Boss drove his pickup back through the desert canyon to the ghost town. In the early morning light, he carried a shovel and the body of Willis Boggins McPherson up the hill to the graveyard where he dug a small hole directly on top of Miss Victoria's resting place. After he covered Willis, the Boss repaired the ground so it once more appeared undisturbed.

Leaning on his shovel, he tried to think of a fitting passage from the Bible, but all that came to him were two words someone had once scribbled in a book of poetry: 'Love endures.' At the time, he wasn't exactly sure what those words meant, but he felt that, in this instance, they fit, and he spoke them aloud, and he felt better for having said them.

## CHAPTER TWELVE

## From Up Here

Sometimes the past can sneak up and surprise you.

Like this one Saturday night I was walking the midway trying to spot trouble before it happened, when I heard a voice call my name. She emerged from the crowd and came straight to me. I didn't recognize her. She wore a headscarf tied under her chin, and she was so very thin, but when she stopped in front of me, she flashed a smile, which told me who she was.

"My God," I said.

"I heard some men in town speak your name. They said you ran things here. I came to see if it was really you."

"I can't believe I ran into you like this," I said.

"I live here."

"In this town? There's nothing around here but desert."

"Yes. Nothing but desert. But when that's all you've got, you learn to live with it."

She reached in her purse and drew out a pack of Camels. Tapping the pack against her hand, she pulled out a single cigarette. She dropped the rest back in her purse and snapped it shut.

When I didn't offer a light, she said, "You used to be more polite."

"I stopped smoking ten years ago."

She reached back in her purse, brought out a lighter and handed it to me. I cupped my hand over the flame, and she leaned into it. She blew smoke at the sky. I closed the lighter, but held it, feeling the warmth against my palm.

She turned her head, coughed once and coughed again. "Are you ill?" I asked.

"I really should quit these things." She took a couple of

more puffs. "Can't help myself."

"There are ways to stop"

"You're concerned about my health now? That's a laugh."

"Just an observation," I said.

She tossed the butt on the ground. "Let's take a walk. It's more comfortable than standing while you stare at me."

"It's just that--I'm shocked to see you. It's been close to ten years."

We began to walk up the midway. On both sides of us, game booths beckoned the rubes. The one that drew the largest crowd was the sharpshooter booth where guys tried to impress their dates by showing their marksmanship. The ping of metal on metal signaled a miss, the clang of metal falling signaled a hit. We heard lots of pings, very few clangs. The sights of our rifles were off a hare to the left, the rifles groves made the bullets fly left.

"Did you get out of Spain before all the trouble begin?" she asked.

"I skipped over to France for a year. Then came home. And you?"

"After what happened between us, I couldn't stay in Europe."

We passed the baseball booth where the rubes tossed softballs at metal bowling pins. It was fixed, too. We placed weights in the balls so they never flew straight. You could have been Babe Ruth himself, and the only way you could knock those pins off the podium was pure luck.

"Can anyone win at the games?' she asked.

"People get lucky sometimes. It can happen."

As if to prove my point, we passed a young couple, the girl admiring a stuffed bear her boyfriend had won for her. We bought them in bulk for twenty-nine cents each, and from the look on the guy's face, I guess he must have plunked down four or five dollars to win it.

"When we were in Spain, you told me you wanted to be a writer," she said. "What happened?"

I shrugged. "I wrote a book. Nobody liked it. So here I am."

"And you own all this," she said.

"I'm the boss. I run the outfit, but I don't own a thing."
"Nothing to tie you down."
"Not really."
"Why should I be surprised?"
"What's that suppose to mean?"
"You know what it means. You know exactly what it means."

I took a deep breath, trying to control my anger. Too often my temper got the best of me, but in this case, I didn't have a right to be angry. "All right, I suppose I know."

"It was a simple operation, you said. And then everything would be like it was before. We could go on with our lives as if nothing had happened."

We passed a concession stand that sold beer. We walked on. I wanted a beer badly.

"Let's not talk about that," I said. "Let's talk about something else. Let's talk about you."

"Me? What do you want to know about me?"

"Did you marry?"

She laughed without humor. "Oh yes. A husband, a house, debts--the full catastrophe."

"But you're alone tonight."

"I'm alone every night."

"Your husband--"

"Gone. I don't know where. I don't care. As for our son--as soon as he was old enough, he left to begin his own life. I said goodbye and good luck. Every now and then, he comes to see me, but it's a chore he does because it's an obligation."

"You don't sound happy."

"Happy?" She reached back in her purse and drew out the Camels. I still held the lighter, and this time without prompting, I lit her cigarette. "I was happy once, a long time ago. At least I thought I was. Then you said I should have the operation, and you promised that everything would be like it was before."

"I thought it would."

"Once you do something like that, nothing can ever be the same again. That was why I left and came home."

"I was wrong. I admit it."

She puffed on the cigarette, smoking it so quickly that it

brought on another coughing spell. She dropped the butt and crushed it with her heel. "I should be smart enough to quit," she said.

We were passing the tent shows now, and Bobby was on stage delivering his come-on for the freak top. She looked at the bannerlines that showed the three-legged man, the pinhead, the wolf boy, the contortionist. "Are they really freaks?" she asked.

"They're just people," I said. "They may look a little different, but their lives are messed up just like everyone else's."

She reached out and touched my arm. "I'm tired now, and I need to go home and go to bed. Before I do, I'd like to take a ride? I'd like to ride the Ferris Wheel. Will you do that with me?"

"Sure."

We walked back up the midway. Because I was the boss, I took her to the front of the line, and once we settled in our seat, the operator snapped the bar across our laps. We began our ascent.

"Do you ride this often," she asked.

"Almost never."

"I'd ride the Ferris Wheel everyday if I could."

We reached the top, and the operator stopped the ride while he let passengers off and seated new ones. The night was warm and clear. She pointed to lights on the far horizon to the west. What's that?" she asked.

"Los Angeles."

"That's sixty miles away. Oh, my, it's so clear--and it looks so close." She lifted her head. "And the stars--they're so bright."

"Up here everything looks far away and up close at the same time," I said.

Far down at the main top, we heard a musical crescendo that signaled the end of an act. Maggie led her female elephant out the rear of the top, their performance over.

"Look. A white Elephant."

I shook my head. "It's a trick of the light. It's gray, an Indian gray."

"Things do look different up here, don't they?"

"Yes, very different."

"The light plays tricks on you."

"Yes. The light plays tricks."

The Wheel began to move again, stopping to let people off and on. We reached the bottom and climbed out. We walked toward the parking lot without saying anything until we reached her car, covered in a fine layer of dust. She unlocked her door, but before she got in, she said, "Are you happy?"

"Once in a while I think I'm happy, but it doesn't last very long."

"Do you ever wonder what our lives would have been like if we if we hadn't--" She fell silent.

"What's the use?" I said. "There's no changing things. Here we are, and that's all there is to it."

"You were a bastard to me." She said it in a matter-of-fact voice.

"I was."

"Are you still a bastard?"

"If you asked some of the people who work for me, they'd say yes."

She slid in the car and started the motor. I thought she was about to drive off, but instead she rolled down the window. "Are you sure the elephant wasn't white?"

"At the time, it just looked that way," I said.

She coughed again, and her body convulsed. Wiping her mouth, she left a dark streak across the back of her hand. She looked at me with eyes recessed so deeply I couldn't see the pupils. "You were a bastard. That was your nature. I knew it when I hooked up with you."

"Did you came here tonight to make me feel guilty?" I asked.

"Maybe." She forced another smile, also humorless. "Maybe I wanted to relive old memories. Maybe I wanted to tell you a deep, dark secret. Maybe I wanted to say goodbye one last time. Maybe it was all of those things. Who the hell knows? Right now I'm too damned tired to figure it out."

She rolled up her window and drove away, a small cloud of dust swirling in her wake.

I went back to the midway and got myself that beer. Afterward, I had another five until I felt a pleasant buzz. I still had trouble sleeping that night. When I woke the next morning and started to dress, I found her lighter in my pants pocket. I didn't have any use for it, so I passed it along to Bobby who ran the freak top.

CHAPTER THIRTEEN

The Last of Benji

Every morning, I swept out the freak top and picked up trash from the night before. The boss in assigning me the job must have seen the choice as ironic, since I'm a hunchback and have a face that remind people of Rondo Hatton, you know, the deformed giant in all those 30's and 40's horror movies like HOUSE OF HORRORS and THE BRUTE MAN. He suffered from an extreme case of acromegalia. I didn't have the disease. I just looked like I had it.

Of course the boss never showed much understanding of irony, so maybe he believed I would fit in better with the freaks and simply tried to do me a kindness. If that was the case, I should have thanked him. From the moment they joined Warbling Brothers Road Show and Circus, I made a whole passel of new friends--Anatol, the three legged man; Vilma the bearded lady; Ruby the contortionist. But my favorites were Mr. Pendergast and his son Benji, who they billed as the Wolf Boy because he had a condition that covered his whole body in hair so thick it looked like fur.

Benji and I hit it off right away. I had just turned twenty-one, and he was a year or so younger. Everyone else connected with Warbling Brothers was in their thirties or older. Benji was a good kid, and his father, who took care of him as well as any father could under the circumstances, had created a swell act that centered around Benji being raised by wolves in the far north before white hunters rescued him. Benji, cloistered in an iron cage especially built for him, had perfected this yell that sounded as real as any wolf call you'd ever heard, and the rubes loved it.

This one morning about three months after Benji and Mr. Pendergast joined us, I went to clean the tent. It was usually a fast job, bagging a few paper cups and napkins the rubes left behind, but the moment I threw back the flap and stepped inside, I saw Benji's cage covered in a thick burlap blanket, but that wasn't what surprised me. Every day around dusk, Mr. Pendergast threw the burlap over the cage and wheeled it backstage. He wouldn't let his son perform at night. I was never sure why except Mr. Pendergast claimed it had to do with Benji's condition.

What caught my attention that morning was Mr. Pendergast. He lay on top of a bedroll next to Benji's cage, one arm under his head. Already past eight, the performers would be setting up in less than an hour, and the rubes would be showing up right after that. People in our profession didn't have the luxury of sleeping late.

I went to wake him. "Mr. Pendergast." I bent over and shook his arm. "You need to get up, Mr. Pendergast. It's getting late."

He didn't open his eyes, and I started to shake him again, but then I saw he wasn't breathing. I kneeled, laid my fingers against his cheek, and found it as cold as a frozen lake. I figured then he must have died early in the night, maybe right after the last show.

"Dali? Is that you?" The muffled voice came from behind the burlap.

Stepping to the front of the cage, I pulled back the cover. Benji crouched inside, his eyes wide with worry. "What are you doing in there?" I asked.

"It's where I sleep." He must have seen the shock registered on my face. "It's because of my condition. The boss knows about it." He gripped the bars leaning into them. "I tried to wake my dad. He's never slept this late." He rattled the bars. "Get me out of here, will you Dali?"

I found a key in the old man's pants' pocket and did as Benji asked. I didn't have the heart to tell him about Mr. Pendergast, but when he stumbled out of the cage, he saw for himself. "Dad," he said.

I laid a hand on his shoulder. "I think he's gone, Benji."

"No." Benji spoke the word as both denial and plea. He sat on the ground and seized his father's hand. "Dad. Dad, wake up."

"You stay here," I told him. "I'll be right back."

I went looking for the boss and found him at the ticket booth passing Becky the cash box. When he saw me, he frowned as if to say if this wasn't damn important, I'd better leave him alone. "What is it?" He growled like an old dog.

"It's Mr. Pendergast. He's dead. I found him by Benji's cage."

His irritation vanished, replaced by an expression of worry. "How?" I shook my head, and he said, "Show me."

We found Benji as I left him, sitting next to his father holding the dead hand. He glanced up at us, the hair on his cheeks glistening with tears.

"Damn it all to hell," the boss said.

For a boss, he wasn't a bad fellow. A couple of times when I asked favors, he did his best to accommodate me, but he was constantly figuring the angles, looking for new ways to bring in fresh revenue. And he didn't like problems because they cost Warbling Brothers money. "What did he die of? Is it contagious?"

"He had a weak heart. For a long time now. It must have given out." Benji turned his head from us, and with the back of his hand, wiped first one hairy cheek, then the other.

At that point, I think the boss was touched by Benji's predicament. He laid a hand on the kid's shoulder. "That's what happens when you put a guy under too much strain. The heart can only take so much."

The boss left us to make a couple of phone calls. I sat beside Benji, who continued to hold his father's hand, and we waited, neither of us speaking. When the boss returned, a couple of cops were with him, and right behind a couple of ambulance drivers pushing a rollaway bed. They said nothing as they picked up Mr. Pendergast and rolled him out of the tent. One of the cops, a big man with a bloated belly, hung back and said to Benji, "Take off your makeup, and you can come with us, kid."

Benji still sat on the ground, his head hung, tears wetting the fur beneath his eyes.

'He's not wearing makeup," I said. "He's got a condition."

"Stupid me, huh?" The cop tried to laugh away his

mistake, but I saw the disgust in his eyes. I had seen that look all my life. "Best you stay here then. Best everybody stay here."

He turned and followed the others from the tent. When he was out of earshot, the boss said, "Bastard." Then to Benji he said, "Don't worry about a thing, kid. I'll see to all the arrangements. You just take care of yourself like your dad would've wanted. Tomorrow before we start breaking camp, we'll have a little get together to honor your dad. You know--a memorial service."

Benji lifted his blood-red eyes to the Boss. "Who's going to take care of me now? What about tonight?"

"Dali here will see to you. You just tell him what you need. Right, Dali?"

"Whatever I can do, Boss," I said.

"And Benji," the boss said. "We need you to go on today. I know it'll be hard, kid, but you can tough it out."

I thought that was pretty raw of the boss to ask that of the kid, but Benji nodded his consent. Maybe he thought work might take his mind off his dad. "You'll stay with me all day?" he asked me. "All day and all night?"

"Like I got somewhere to go," I said.

The freak show was a ten for one, ten acts for the price of one. It had a bare stage, and each act got its time on the hardwood. They saved Benji for last because that way we left customers scratching their heads and talking to themselves. They had never seen anything like him. His father would wheel the cage on stage, and with it still covered, tell the audience this fantastic story of hunters finding Benji running with the wolves. Then he would throw off the cover, and Benji would let out his patented wolf call. On this day, I substituted for Mr. Pendergast, telling the story as best I could to a tent three-fourths full. When I threw back the burlap, Benji gave out his wolf impersonation, but this time it was far different from anything I'd ever heard. He sang a song with that call, a song of loneliness and dispair that ripped into your gut and made you feel what he must have felt. I'd never heard anything like it before or since, and it hurt to the core, like it was me that was suffering. When I looked at the audience, I could see by their expressions they felt the same as I, and more than one woman began to cry.

I dropped the cover back over the cage. It wasn't good

what had happened. One rule of carny life says you could cheat the rubes, you could scare them, you could fool them all you want, but never make them cry. Never.

Yet when the next show started, the rubes filled the place from side to side, front to back. By the third show, there were so many that the sides of the tent bulged outward. By then, when I threw back the cover and Benji let out his cry, my own tears flowed. That's how deep his song cut.

After the seven o'clock show, Benji said, "You better take me backstage. It's almost dark."

I did as he instructed, setting the cage in its usual resting place. "Now lock me in," he said.

"I don't feel right about that. I mean--you've been in that thing all night and all day. Don't you want to stretch your legs?"

"Just lock me in. Please."

I still had the key in my pocket from that morning, and once more I did as he asked. He reached through the bars and rattled the lock to make sure it was secure. "Cover me now. Make sure no one comes to look."

I dropped the burlap, shutting him off from the world. "Can I get you anything?"

"In the morning," he said. "Just don't go anywhere. Stay with me."

"I'll be right here, Benji."

The bedroll, the one I found Mr. Pendergast on, still lay beside the cage, and I sat down to wait out the night. The rest of the acts went through two more shows, but I could tell from the responses that the crowds had thinned considerably. I carried a book with me at all times, and right then I was in the middle of Balzac's *Lost Illusions*. By the end of the last show, I had finished the book. After that, I dropped back on the bedroll and dozed off.

Around one in the morning I awoke to the whines of an animal. They came from inside the cage. The lights from the midway penetrated the walls of the tent enough for me to see. I sat up and pulled back the corner of the burlap.

A body huddled on the far side of the cage, but it wasn't Benji. Instead it was a creature with a stout instead of a nose, paws and claws instead of hands and feet, fangs instead of teeth. It slept and dreamed, but the dreams were nightmares, and it cried out. Waking itself, it opened its eyes and glared at me, red eyes, eyes of a creature older than man himself. Maybe I should've been afraid, but I wasn't.

It crept across the floor on all fours until his face rested against the bars, and I smelled his fetid breath that spoke of wild forests and prairies, of mountains and meadows, of the steaming entrails of a kill. It growled, but it sounded plaintive rather than threatening. A brown paw worked its way through the bars, and I reached out and took it. A few minutes later, the creature fell back asleep.

The next day just as the boss promised, we held a memorial service for Benji's father. The boss hired a local Baptist minister who delivered the service from the bare stage. When he first looked out at us, he must have gotten quite a shock. There were Benji and me sitting in the front row, others of our kind gathered round. Then there were the roustabouts and the barkers and the circus performers. I'm sure he never had an audience like ours, but we remained quiet and respectful right to the end. Since he didn't know Mr. Pendergast, the minister had little to say beyond a few clichés including "he's in a better place" crap.

Afterward, the boss gave Benji the rest of day off. We were breaking down the show, getting ready to move to the next town. The boss had me check on Benji half a dozen times during the day. Once he asked how the kid was doing. "He's pretty broken up," I said.

"You're keeping him happy, ain't you, Dali?"

"As best I can, but I'm not his father," I said.

Two days later we set up in Simi Valley. By then I could see the kid wasn't feeling any better. I saw it in his haggard face and his thinning body. Often during the day I caught him staring off at the grassy mountains that surrounded us. At lunch I sat with him at the Pie Wagon. "What's going on, Benji?" I asked.

He stared at his food as if it disgusted him. "My condition--it's getting worse. Without Dad, I can't control it. Maybe I don't want to control it."

That evening just before dusk, I rolled his cage backstage, and he asked me to let him out. "I need to go to the pot before I turn in," he said.

When he didn't come back after half an hour, I went looking for him. I found his clothes folded and abandoned next to an Andy Gump.

None of us ever saw him again, and for a while, the boss was damned angry at me for letting him get away. But like I told him, Benji had a right to live the way he wanted. About a week later, I read in the LOS ANGELES TIMES that a local Simi Valley rancher blamed a wolf for the deaths a couple of his sheep. He swore he saw the creature one night. "Big as a man," he said, "loping along on all fours."

I knew then that at least Benji was in a better place. He was free of cages and running with wind. I envied him.

## CHAPTER FOURTEEN

## Pug

The young guy from Escondido swung me by the arm and let go. I tumbled through the ropes and ended up on the floor sprawled on my back. I groaned, trying to push myself up on my elbows, sawdust clinging to my sweaty back and arms. I shook my head and spit out a glob of blood. The ref began to count: one, two, three, four--
  Of course, it was fake. The kid had paid off the Boss so I would throw the fight. The blood was a small capsule of food coloring I bit into. All had gone according to rehearsal until that point, when out of nowhere, two hands seized me under my arms and hauled me to my feet. This I hadn't expected. The kid was the hometown hero, I the outsider, the villain. What poor sucker would help me? The guy whispered in my ear, "You're doing just fine, Red."
  I looked over my shoulder and saw this guy with a crooked nose and a wide smile. He stood an inch or so taller than me, his body much thinner. Something about him seemed familiar. I was always running into guys I'd served with in the army, some I knew well, others only passing acquaintances, others who remembered me from my matches. I figured he was one of the latter.
  His interference didn't matter. The next part of our act had me getting back into the ring, which I did, struggling to grab a rope and hauling myself up. The kid--he couldn't have been more than nineteen--came running at me. I got him in a headlock and pretended to gouge his eyes. The audience booed. He fell against the turnbuckle, I went after him, he landed an uppercut with his forearm, and I dropped. He pinned me for the count of three, and the ref raised his hand in victory as the crowd applauded and cheered.

From the canvas, I watched a girl climb up on the ringside and plant a long, wet kiss on the kid. Arm in arm, they went back to one of the dressing rooms. She was a good-looking brunette with soft brown eyes. I envied him. I still had another two matches before I could call it a day, and by then, even if a woman fell into my lap, I'd be too tired to do anything about it.

That's the way things went when you worked an athletic show in a carnival as I did back in '48 for Warbling Brothers Road Show and Circus. Mostly the matches were on the up and up, and frankly with my knowledge of martial arts, none of the cowboys or farmers stood much of a chance against me, not unless they paid to fix the outcome, like the kid had done that night. Guys usually thought they could handle me. I was only five eight, and my build was no better than average. Most of the guys I wrestled towered over me and had muscles in places I didn't even know you could have muscles.

But on that particular weekend, things had gotten pretty rough. Ordinarily we had two other muscle-heads--the carny's name for guys like me--another wrestler and a boxer, but the wrestler left the past month to join the pro circuit, and on the same day, the boxer took a legitimate tumble out of the ring and broke his collarbone. That left only me to handle all comers, and I was going through nine and sometimes ten bouts a day. No matter how good a guy is, getting pounded that often is going to wear you down.

As I dragged myself back to the dressing room, I glanced around for the Samaritan who helped me to my feet, but I didn't see him in the crowd surging for the exit. I didn't think much more about him. In my dressing room, I poured myself a glass of water and rinsed my mouth of the food coloring. That was about all the strength I had. I flopped on the cot, not bothering to wash up. By that time, I had wrestled five matches in five hours, and even though the last was fixed, I was dogged tired, every muscle and bone crying for rest. In the dressing room next to mine separated by a thin canvas wall, I heard the kid and girl moaning and groaning like the world was coming to an end, but even that couldn't keep me from falling asleep.

I awoke with the Boss standing over me, shaking my shoulder. Swinging my legs over the cot, I came to my feet instantly alert, the result of my years in the Marines, a habit I hadn't yet broken. The Boss wasn't alone. Next to him stood the guy who helped me off the floor.

"He says he knows you," the Boss said.

The guy held out his hand, and I took it. But he must have seen my hesitation as I searched his face trying to remember. "Pug," he said. "Everybody called me Pug."

I remembered him then as he used to be, as slick and smooth a boxer as you've ever seen, all lean, hard muscle and lighting quick with his gloves. "You've lost a lot weight," I said.

"I can still box." He sniffed heavily like he had trouble breathing through his nose, which I suspect he did. It looked as if it had been broken more than once and never set properly. He jabbed the air a couple of times, throwing in that little twist at the end that gave his punches such power.

"Wants to join the show," the Boss said. "What about it? Can he box? He said you'd know."

"Back in '43, while we were stationed at Pearl Harbor, I saw him fight half a dozen times. I never saw him lose once."

Grinning, Pug nodded. "Before the war, I fought in the Garden. Fought Baby Duarte. Remember him? He was going to be the next middleweight champion of the world." He jabbed the air again, his fist flashing--swish, swish, swish. "Third round, I caught him with a right hook to the sternum, and an uppercut to the chin. They had to pick him up and carry him to his corner. He lived up to his nickname that night. He was crying like a baby."

"I heard you went back to ring after the war," I said. "What happened?"

He shrugged. "The fighting game has changed. Too many crooks. They all want their cut, and if you don't go along, you don't fight." Maybe he started to leave it at that, and maybe he saw my face, that I didn't really believe him. He said, "Look, I'm thirty-one years old. For a professional fighter, I'm an old man. Promoters don't want me. They want young kids who'll pound themselves silly. They want blood and guts. They don't want boxers. They want brawlers. Me, I'm a boxer. Always have been, always will be."

"Enough with the life story. You're making me cry," the

Boss said. "I just want to know if I should hire this guy. What about it?"

The Boss put me in a rough spot. I mean, here he was asking me whether or not he should hire Pug with the guy standing right in front of me. But the way I remembered Pug, the answer wasn't hard at all. "He was as good a boxer as I've ever seen," I said.

The Boss nodded to Pug. "I'll set up a match for later tonight. If you pass muster, you got a job."

Sure enough the Boss managed to find a big bruiser who stood six feet and must have outweighed Pug by seventy-five pounds. He paid for the privilege, ten dollars, the going rate for a fight that wasn't fixed. Even if the guy wanted to fix it, I doubt the Boss would have agreed. He wanted to see what Pug had. As tired as I was, I stayed awake to see Pug, too.

He didn't disappoint. The big guy came out swinging wildly, trying to land a quick knockout. Pug sidestepped, jabbed, and back-peddled, forcing the big guy to chase him. By the middle of the second round, the guy could barely hold up his hands, huffing and puffing like a dying asthmatic. Pug delivered two swift blows to the midsection, and the bruiser went down on all fours. The guy got to his feet and staggered a few steps before Pug caught him with two hard hooks to the face. This time when the guy hit the canvas, he stayed down for the count.

Back in the dressing room, Pug dropped in a chair, and I helped remove his gloves. "Damn, that was good, Red," he said. "I haven't hit anybody in so long, I'd forgotten how good it feels. I still got it, don't I, Red? I still got it."

His face was flushed and full of blotches. Small blood vessels streaked his nose like blue lightening. For the first time, I smelled his whiskey breath, although he had tried to disguise with sen-sen. "You've been drinking," I said.

He shrugged. "I had a little snort before the match. You know, to settle my nerves."

"Don't give me that baloney, Pug. Back in '43, if you landed body blows like you did on that fellow tonight, he'd never gotten off the mat."

He leaned forward, his elbows on his knees, and stared at the floor. "Okay, I drink a little."

"Not a little, Pug." I tossed the gloves in a corner. "What's going on?"

"Did I ever tell you I was at Iwo Jima? That was a tough one, Red."

I knew a lot of guys like Pug who still remembered the war like it was yesterday and felt they were going back tomorrow. Most of them drank to dull the pain, to help them forget, to help them make it from one day to the next. I had never seen one minute of actual combat, so who was I to judge? I said, "That stuff will kill you, Pug. It's no good."

He nodded without looking up. "You won't tell the Boss, will you? I'd like to keep the job."

"The Boss isn't dumb. He'll figure it out sooner or later unless you lay off the sauce."

He closed his hands together like a man in prayer. "I can do that."

And he did for a while. The next night, Pug fought three matches, winning each with relative ease. At the end of the night in his dressing room, he hopped around jabbing the air like he was still in the ring. "They barely laid a glove on me, Red," he said. "Those big palookas couldn't catch me. I still got my speed, my quickness. Ain't that right, Red."

"You're the champ," I said. "The best I've ever seen."

He stopped suddenly and faced me, his expression sober. "You mean I *was* the best."

"You were best out there tonight," I said, "and that's what counts."

Monday came, and the show packed up and moved on. Pug bunked with me in a trailer along with two other performers, the Coen Brothers, Saul and Samuel, trapeze artists and émigrés from Germany. They spoke English fluently, and they wanted to know everything about America. They thought Pug fascinating, and every night before bed, the three would sit around the table while Pug told them stories of the boxing game. After the first night I didn't pay much attention, having heard such stories from Pug and other pugilists like him, but Saul and Samuel couldn't get enough.

By Thursday evening, we were up and running again in Temecula in celebration of the city's Wild West Days. Pug and I didn't have any matches the first night, but the boss lined up bouts for Friday. Once more Pug boxed circles around his opponents, winning all his matches with far more ease than I won mine. He was in the pink. He was on top of the world.

That night, well past midnight and long after I fell into a deep sleep, exhausted, I awoke to Pug screaming. "No! God, no! Jimmy! Jimmy! Jimmy!"

I sat up as did the Coen brothers, all three of us instantly awake. I reached under my bed for the flashlight I always kept there, and pushing the button, I shot a beam of light across the room. Pug sat up in bed, awakened by his own screams. He stared into the light, his eyes wide with terror, his face covered in sweat. "Jimmy?" he said. "Is that you, Jimmy?"

I went to him, laying a hand on his shoulder. "It's me. Red." I shifted the light so that he could see my face. "You know where you are, Pug?" He nodded once, although I could see remnants of doubt and fear buried in his eyes. "You having the DT's?" I asked.

He ran his fingers through thinning, damp hair. "A bad dream."

Saturday night after Pug's last bout, he and the Coen brothers disappeared. Along about one in the morning, Saul and Samuel dragged him home. The door opened, Saul stepped through, and Samuel passed Pug to him. The brothers were on the diminutive side, each less than five five in height, each weighing less than a hundred twenty. Their waists were thinner than most women's. Together they half carried, half dragged Pug to his bed. Pug was snoring even before he hit the mattress.

"We just went out for one beer." Saul held up his index as if it proved his point. "Only one, I told him. Samuel and I cannot afford more. In fact, neither of us finished our beer. But Pug, he drank and drank. We tried to get him to stop, but he would not listen."

"Drunks never do," I said.

Samuel wrung his hands as if he thought he and his brother were in trouble. "What must we do now? Should we tell the Boss?"

"Let him sleep it off," I said.

In the morning I awoke to find the brothers sitting at Pug's bedside, watching as he snored. I dressed and brushed my teeth. Afterward I filled a glass with water, took three aspirins out of the medicine chest and went to Pug's bedside. I leaned over and shook him until he opened his eyes. Light streamed in from a window, the early morning sun casting deep shadows in the lines and crevices of his face, making him appear fifteen years older than he was. He held a hand up to shade his eyes. I offered the glass and aspirins.

"Thanks," he said, his voice barely a whisper.

He downed the aspirin, and I took the glass back, laying it on a table next to the bed. "You need the cure."

Smiling, he sat up. "I had a couple of beers is all."

"Should I tell the Boss you can't make it tonight?" I asked.

"Hey--" He drew the word out like I came to the wrong conclusions. "I'm fine."

He fought four matches that night, one every hour beginning at six. The first was fixed, so he didn't expend much energy. I watched the seven o'clock match. Like most of these farmers and ranchers, his opponent was a big, lumbering guy who chased Pug around the ring. Pug did his best to dodge and weave his way out of trouble, but the fellow landed a couple of wild swings that staggered Pug. Pug won the match as well as his eight o'clock, but by then he had absorbed another half dozen blows to his head and body. Back in the dressing room, he could barely catch his breath. He sat in a chair, holding his elbows into his ribs, his flesh red with rising welts.

Right then I went to the Boss, finding him walking the midway as he usually did, trying to stop trouble before it began. I told him I didn't think Pug could go on.

The Boss followed me back to the dressing room, but before we reached it, we saw Pug, still dressed in his trunks, a robe thrown over his shoulders, weaving his way toward an Andy Gump. He halted, dropped on all fours and spewed a stream of brown bile into the dust. We ran to help, but by the time we reached him, Pug was on his feet, wiping his mouth with the back of his hand. The stink of puke pervaded the air, and silently as if in agreement, the three of us moved back to the athletic top.

In the dressing room, the Boss said, "What the hell's going on?"

"Something I ate." Pug patted his belly. "Nothing to worry about, Boss."

"Can you go on?"

Pug glanced at me and nodded. "I'm fine now."

The Boss pushed his lips together, and turning, said, "I want to talk to you."

I followed him outside. There behind the top, we stopped, hidden in deep shadows so that I couldn't see his face. He said, "He's an alkie. I should have seen it the day he hired on. But he was a friend of yours, so I thought he'd be okay."

"Had I known, Boss, I would've told you."

"I should fire his ass right now." For a moment he said nothing, the only sounds those of the midway. At last he said, "You tell him, he falls off the wagon again, he's gone. Make sure he understands." He spoke without anger. I think he must have known guys like Pug, just as I had, and he had a soft spot for them, too, but he ran a business. Sentiment and business don't mix. He meant what he said. He wouldn't like firing Pug, but he would if he had to.

I went back inside and found Pug waiting for me. "Do I still have a job?" he asked, and I told him what the Boss said. "It's just that when I dream, it's like I'm back there. I get a snoot full, I don't dream. I can sleep then."

"You have many more nights like tonight, you'll be crawling in the ring."

"Yeah. You're right. I need to lay off the sauce. I can do that."

For the next two weeks as we traveled from city to city, he drank cokes and smoked and cursed, but as far as I saw, he never once touched beer or liquor. But his dreams worsened. Two and three times a night he would jump up screaming, his body covered in sweat, and when that happened, he woke us all. One morning Saul and Samuel came to me, and Saul said, "Your friend, he wakes us up at all hours. We are always tired. This we cannot afford. Our act depends upon timing. You understand? Split second timing. If we are tired, if we have had no sleep, we become careless."

"What do you want me to do?" I asked.

Samuel wrung his hands. "We like your friend. We have nothing against him."

Saul's brow darkened. "The Boss has found us other quarters."

"It is nothing personal," Samuel said. "We just need our sleep."

And so they deserted us, and left me to my own little purgatory. Like Pug, I began to dread the nights, knowing that without doubt, his dreams would frighten and awake me, just as they did him. Soon I began to wonder if a drink or two might settle my nerves and allow me to get a good night's sleep.

Pug fell off the wagon again in Pomona. After the midway closed, I spent a little time with Millie, one of the circus performers, and when I got back to the trailer and saw Pug wasn't there, I went looking for him.

Sure enough, I found him two blocks from the midway. He sat alone at the far end of a bar nursing an empty whiskey glass and a beer chaser. He watched me walk over to him, but his gaze seemed unfocused. The bartender came to ask me what I wanted. "How many has he had?" I asked.

"I cut him off half an hour ago," he said. "He's been nursing that beer ever since."

"I need one more." Hunched over the bar like an old man stricken with rheumatism, he turned his deep-set eyes on me, the bags under them hanging like rotten bananas. "Please, Red, just one more."

"Pour him one more," I said to the bartender, and sat on the stool next to Pug. "Pour me one while you're at it."

Pug downed his in one quick swallow. I took a sip and left the rest untouched. What the hell was I thinking? I asked myself. I didn't even like the stuff.

I helped Pug back to the trailer and put him to bed. Except for his snoring, he slept soundly the whole night and late into the morning.

He managed a couple of weeks before he went on another bender, only this time the Boss brought him back. After Pug sobered up the next morning, the Boss came to our trailer. Pug sat on the side of the bed, his hands folded together, his head bowed. "You're a drunk," the Boss told him. "You're a fall down, stinking drunk. You need help. You need to take the cure. Otherwise, I can't use you."

Pug lifted his bloodshot eyes. "If I take the cure--?"

"You take the cure, I won't fire you. You're a good muscle-head. I'll keep a place for you." He lifted his finger, leveling it at Pug. "You better come back prepared to stay on the wagon for good."

"I can do that," Pug said.

The next day we packed up the show and moved on. About three in the afternoon, we passed Claremont. The caravan proceeded on to Bakersfield while I drove Pug to the Claremont Clinic, right next to the college. I checked him in and helped him settle in his room. He sat in a chair, his elbows on his knees, his hands gripped together. "You won't forget me, Red?" he said.

I laid my hand on his shoulder. "I'll call every chance I get--at least once a week. I promise. You'll only be here three months. Ninety days. Then it'll all be over. Next month, we'll be in Montclair. That's only a few miles down the highway. I'll come by and see you then."

His eyes watered, and with a quick wave, I said goodbye and hurried out the door.

Certainly I intended to keep my word to call as often I promised. I did call him that first week, and he told me he thought the cure was working. "Already I don't crave the sauce like I used to," he said. "I'm feeling a hundred times better. In another week or two, I'll be in the pink."

After that, I simply forgot to call. The Boss had me wrestling six to eight matches a night each Friday and Saturday, and I was too worn out to do anything but spend the rest of the time recuperating. Then over a month later, we rolled into Montclair. I told the Boss I was going to see Pug. "When you come back, I want the truth," he said. "I don't want you lying for him. I want to know exactly how he's doing."

Half an hour later, I stood before the check-in desk facing a starched uniform nurse. When I told her I wanted to see Pug--Mr. Pugnassy--she excused herself and hurried off down the hall. She returned a minute later with a heavy-set woman dressed in civilian clothes. I recognized her as the head administrator who had checked Pug in. "You've come to see Mr. Pugnassy. Please, come me to my office. We can talk there."

I figured she was going to tell me Pug had fallen off the wagon. I had hoped for better, but I couldn't say I was surprised. I dropped by butt in an overstuffed chair as she took a seat behind her desk.

"Did Mr. Pugnassy have any relatives?" she asked.

The story was simple. The cure worked, and Pug dried out, his system cleaning itself. But he had dreams--nightmares--they couldn't control. "Our doctors did everything they could," she assured me. "We took precautions, but--he just didn't have the will power."

When I got back, the Boss asked, "Well?"

"We cured him," I said.

It wasn't all my fault. Both the Boss and I convinced Pug to take the cure, but in doing so, we had taken away his only means of endurance. The woman blamed Pug for his lack of will power, but that wasn't what killed him. It wasn't his drinking either. Nightmares killed Pug. Sure, the Boss and I only wanted to help, but we should have remembered that sometimes helping a guy is the worse thing you can do for him.

CHAPTER FIFTEEN

The Death of Fluggie

Pookie the Geek, staring to feel good, half the bottle of Ripple already pumping through his bloodstream, staggered from the freak top on his way to the portable head. Passing between two flatbed trucks, he tripped and almost fell. Because his bladder felt as if it were about to burst, he hurried on.

Once he closed the door and unbuttoned his pants, he peed for what seemed like five minutes, so long that by the time he stepped back outside, he had forgotten his walk over. He did remember the bottle tucked under his arm, and uncorking it, took a long drink. On his return to the freak top, he once more passed between the trucks, and once more tripped. This time, unable to right himself, he slammed to the ground with such force the bottle flew from his hand. Stunned, he lay in the dirt until his head cleared and he could push himself to his elbows. Wine soaked the ground, turning it a red so dark it appeared black. Seizing the bottle, he righted it and held it to the light. Only a small residue clung to the bottom. "Awwww--no," he groaned. He sat up, propping his back against a wheel of the flatbed. Lifting the bottle, he drained the last drops. Afterward he licked the rim.

That was when he saw two oversized red shoes with toes that curled back on themselves sticking out from under the flatbed. Pookie peered around the tire, and there lay Fluggie the Clown, his head tilted toward Pookie. Pookie leaned over and grabbed Fluggie by one of his clown shoes. Except for the leg that Pookie shook, Fluggie refused to move. Pookie gave up and patted the clown on the ankle. "You's really drunk, Mister Clown. The Boss gonna fire your ass if he find out."

The clown looked at him with wide, unflinching eyes, and the idea struck Pookie that maybe Fluggie wasn't sleeping it off. Maybe the poor bastard was sick. Using the rim of the tire for support, Pookie climbed to his feet and came to get me.

I was still in my trailer resting from the last show of the day. I was the caller--the barker--for the freak top, and even though Pookie was an out and out drunk, I liked the little guy. In those days, summer '48, he was the only Negro performer we had at Warbling Brothers Road Show and Circus, although half a dozen worked as roustabouts. Pookie was full of stories, and I spent more time with him than anybody else. I don't guess he had another friend but me. Still, he never once came to my dressing room because I was a young white guy, and I suppose he would have felt out of place.

So when he threw open the door without knocking, he surprised me. I was listening to "I Love a Mystery", and I looked up, angry for the interruption. "What the hell, Pookie?" I said.

"I think you better come quick, Mister Bobby. Fluggie the Clown is out there under one of them trucks. He don't look so good."

Fluggie was part of a husband-wife act, Willie and Myrna Sanford, the two of them having been with Warbling Brothers the past five years or so. There was a third wheel in the cog, Rosa Vasquez, one of the girls who worked the hoochie kooch. The three of them shared the same trailer. "He's been hitting the sauce lately," I said. "Maybe he's just sleeping it off."

"That's what I thought at first." Pookie gripped the door jam to steady himself. "Then I gots to thinking maybe it was something else. I thinks you better come and see."

I pulled a flashlight from one of the drawers.

Even though I liked Pookie, cheap liquor warped his judgment. For all I knew, Pookie had suffered a bad dream, and I might be on a fool's errand. Still, if Fluggie had tied one on, I couldn't leave him lying out there all night. The Big Top and midway had closed an hour before, and the next day we were packing up and leaving. Somebody might decide to move the truck, and if that happened, the show would be minus one clown.

Pookie led me to the red shoes stickling out from under the flatbed. I squatted and aimed the flashlight. Willie, still in his Fluggie getup, lay with his eyes open, a painted grin spread across his face.

"He ain't drunk, is he?" said Pookie.

I stood. "You wait here, Pookie. I'm going to get the Boss."

I interrupted the Boss counting the nightly take. He wasn't any happier than I at being disturbed, but when I told him we had trouble, he locked his trailer and came with me. Together we climbed under the truck and took a long look at Fluggie. Blood caked the back of his red wig and turned the sawdust around his head into a thick, red mix. He shaved his head because the wig was so hot, and when I parted the fake hair, I found a very deep and dark indentation in the back of his skull.

The Boss took the flashlight from me and tilted it at Pookie, who blinked and held his hand up to shield his eyes. "What do you know about this, Pookie?" the Boss asked.

Pookie shook his head, his expression one of disappointment and hurt. "I don't know nothing, Boss. I just coming back from the head. That when I tripped over Fluggie. That's when I came to get Mister Bobby."

The Boss crawled out from under the truck and stood. "Let me see your hands."

Pookie held out his hands palms up. The Boss turned the light on them, and satisfied, said, "I had to check, Pookie. It's not that I don't trust you, but if people asked--" He shrugged. "You understand."

"Yes sir, I guess I do." Pookie dropped his hands to his side.

For the next five minutes, we searched the nearby ground looking for the weapon. From the wound, I guessed a hammer--not a fancy one, just a plain old hammer--but we didn't find anything. The Boss dropped down on one knee to inspect the soft dirt. "He made it here on his own," he said.

"How the hell could he do that?" I asked.

"You'd be surprised what a guy can do after he's been hurt." The Boss stood and flicked off the flashlight, burying the three of us in deep shadows. "I've seen guys with all sorts of injuries do crazy things, including this one guy who got half his skull get blown off and still managed to walk all the way to a hospital. Died on his feet just as the doctors got to him." He glanced down at Fluggie. "People hold on for as long as they can."

"What do we do now?" I asked.

"Let's take care of Fluggie. We don't anyone else stumbling over him. Then we'll go see his wife and that girl--the one who moved in with them."

"Rosa," I said.

"Yeah--her."

We wrapped Fluggie, costume and all, in a blanket the Boss brought from his trailer, and together, the three of us hauled the body to the pie wagon, a big truck in which we carried our food and from which the cooks prepared our meals. We stored our perishable goods like meats and milk in a locker full of blocks of ice. We found an empty corner where we laid Fluggie.

The Boss closed the truck, locking the doors to the storage. By then, Pookie had sobered up, his face drawn and haggard, the lines across his forehead and cheeks so deep he looked a hundred years old, even though he was no more than forty. "You go on to bed, Pookie," the Boss told him.

"I'm out of hooch." Pookie's voice shook like a man having the chills.

The Boss dug in his pocket and came up with two bits. "This is for coffee, not liquor. There's an all night café down the street. Sober up and don't say anything about this, you hear?"

"I don't even want to think about it." Pookie took the twenty-five cents and wandered off into the dark. The Boss asked, "Can he keep quiet?"

"Pookie may be a drunk, but he'll do what you tell him," I said.

"Then come on. Let's go see the wife and the girl." He stepped off, his boots kicking up dust.

Reaching the Sanford's trailer van, we heard a woman crying inside. The Boss knocked, his knuckles rapping the metal. The door swung open, and there stood Rosa. Every time I saw her, my chest ached like a hundred pound rock was pressing against it. She was good-looking--there was no denying that--although she wasn't beautiful, not in the classic way like some of the other girls who worked the hoochie koochie. Instead she exuded a raw sexuality. Her full lips seemed made for kissing, and she carried a more than ample bosom accentuated by her thin waist. She wore her black hair braided so it hung almost to her hips, and when she walked, it swayed like rope blowing in the wind. She had a way of looking at a man with those deep brown eyes that made him feel like he was the only one in the world, and that made her especially desirable for the hoochie kooch. Guys drooled over her, and more than once, fights had broken out during her performance.

She looked at us now with those brown eyes blazing with a controlled fury as if she were mad at the world, and since we were there, she would take it out on us. "What you want?" She spit the words at us, her Mexican accent thick and heavy.

"We came to see about Fluggie," the Boss said, and then catching himself, he said, "Willie--I mean Willie."

"He ain't here." Rosa started to slam the door, but the Boss caught the handle. Angrily Rosa said, "I told you, he ain't here. Now leave us alone."

"I know he's not here," the Boss said. "We found him lying under one of the trucks."

"Yeah, well he can stay there," Rosa said.

The Boss pushed the door wider and stepped into the trailer with me right behind. There at the kitchen table sat Myrna, Fluggie's wife. It was funny. I knew him as Willie Sanford--I called him Willie--but now for some reason, I could think of him only as Fluggie.

Like her husband, Myrna still wore her clown makeup, the baggy costume, the wild, red wig, the turned up red shoes, and also like her husband, a painted smile that covered half her face, but she wasn't happy. She held a wadded up, bloody tissue in her hand. Long streaks of smeared grease paint hung under her eyes. Her left cheek was swollen, her eye almost closed.

I tapped the Boss on the arm and drew his attention to the countertop of the sink. There lay a hammer, the blunt end bright with fresh blood. "What happened, Ladies?" the Boss asked.

"That husband of hers complain to you?" Rosa stood in the middle of the kitchen, her hands on her hips. "You tell him to go to hell. We don't need him any more. Tell him to stay out of our lives."

"Who cracked him with the hammer?"

"I did," Rosa said. "He comes back, I do it again."

"Why?" I asked.

She glared at me with those brown eyes. "Look at Myrna's face. And look at her neck. Go ahead, Myrna. Show them your neck."

Myrna lifted her chin and we could see the greasepaint under her neck, large fingerprints embedded among the yellow and black. "He was killing her," Rosa said.

"Over what?" the Boss asked.

Myrna reached out, and Rosa took her hand, stepping in close.

"That's what I thought," said the Boss.

"You tell the bastard to stay away," Rosa said. "You tell him not ever to come around here again."

"He won't be coming back," the Boss said. "Not ever."

At first neither woman reacted. Then simultaneously, they both grasped his meaning, their eyes widening. The Boss told them of finding Fluggie. Myrna began to cry again, her sobs wracking her body.

"You calling the cops?" Rosa asked. The anger had drained from her voice.

"Fluggie was one of us, and the cops got no part in it," the Boss said.

Rosa looked down at Myrna. "I just wanted him to stop hurting you."

Myrna leaned into Rosa, her arms circling the girl's waist. Her face smeared greasepaint on Rosa's blue skirt, but neither appeared to notice or care.

We left them, and the Boss told me to come with him. Once more we moved Fluggie, the two of us dragging him from behind the blocks of ice and carrying him through the shadows to the Boss' trailer where we stored him in the bottom of a closet. Afterward he told me to go find Pookie and make sure the geek was sober in the morning. The three of us had to take care of this.

"You going to sleep here with the dead guy?" I asked.

"It ain't the dead that scares me," he said.

The next day the crew began to dismantle the shows and midways. We were moving on to Indio, close to a hundred miles to the east. The Boss told everyone we would meet them there, and just past seven, Pookie and I climbed in the front seat of the Boss' truck, his trailer hooked on behind. Sliding behind the wheel, he started the motor, shifted into low, and pulled out into the street. Myrna and Rosa followed in their van.

Somewhere near Palm Springs, the Boss turned off the main highway and followed a small two-lane road up through the canyons until it became dirt ruts. By then it was near ten o'clock, and the day was beginning to heat up. I wondered how long Fluggie would keep under such conditions. We were all sweating pretty good by the time the Boss turned the truck and trailer into a wide spot near half a dozen tumbled down cabins. Holes and mounds of dirt and rotted timber dotted the hillsides. Myrna and Rosa pulled in right behind us, a cloud of dust rolling in with them.

Pookie and I dragged the corpse from the trailer, and by the time we were outside, the Boss was standing twenty or thirty yards away next to a hole that had timber strung over it and a hoist to remove the diggings. Heat waves shimmered, making the Boss appear more mirage than real.

With Myrna and Rosa tagging along behind, Pookie and I carried Fluggie across the open ground and laid the body close to the hole. By then Pookie was shaking pretty badly. He needed his bottle, but as the Boss instructed, I made sure he was sober, and he had to do without until this thing was finished.

The Boss picked up a rock the size of his fist and tossed it into the hole. We never heard it hit bottom. Ordinarily a hole so deep emitted cool air, but not this one. A wind blew up the canyon, and heat swirled around us like we were in the middle of a furnace. "No telling how deep this old mine shaft is," the Boss said. "Once Fluggie goes in, he's there for good. Anybody got anything to say?"

"Yeah," said Rosa. "Good riddance."

The Boss scratched his chin, his nails clicking against dark stubble. "Anybody got anything good to say."

"He brought me a cup of java once." Pookie held his hands together to keep them from shaking. "I could sure use one now."

We all looked at each other, waiting for someone else to speak. Finally I said, "He was a good clown. He knew his business."

Myrna nodded and dabbed her eyes with a tissue.

"I guess that's all there is," said the Boss. He motioned to Pookie and me.

I grabbed the body by the shoulders, Pookie by the feet. I said to Pookie. "On the count of three."

We began to swing the body as I counted. "One--two--"

On three, we let go. Fluggie dropped, and like the rock before him, we never heard him hit bottom.

The Boss faced the women who clung to each other, Myrna still crying, Rosa standing straight, looking the Boss in the eye. "What you going to do? Toss us in the hole, too?" Rosa said.

The Boss ignored her. "From now on, if anyone asks, this is the story, and we all stick to it. One day Fluggie walked away, just like that--" He snapped his fingers. "--and he never came back. None of us knows what happened. That's all we have to say, and no one can prove anything different."

"And that's it? Nothing happens to us?" Rosa asked.

"Not quite," said the Boss. "You're fired. Both of you. Get in your van, go where you want, just don't let me see you again."

"You're firing us?" Rosa sounded incredulous. "It wasn't our fault. He tried to kill Myrna--"

"Of course it's your fault," the Boss said. "You two didn't mean to kill him--I believe that--but you own just as much blame as him. If you can't see that, you're blind."

Rosa started to protest again, but Myrna squeezed her hand, silencing her. "Don't, please. Just let's go," she said.

We watched the women drive away, clouds of dust rising behind them. We walked back to the Boss's truck and climbed in the front seat. Pookie sat between us, shaking so badly his knee kept knocking against the gear shift. The Boss said, "It's all over Pookie. As soon as we get to Indio, we'll get you a bottle."

I looked up the road just as the trailer van disappeared around a bend, dust from it wake lingering in the canyon. "Where do you think they'll go?" I asked.

"Hell if I know," said the Boss. "Hell if I care. They don't belong to us anymore."

CHAPTER SIXTEEN

The Artistry of Wild Bill Saunders

Wild Bill Saunders decided to kill his wife Marie during their act on stage.

Before we get to that, let me tell you about Wild Bill. A handsome devil he was, standing a good six feet and built like a blond Greek god in the years before body building became popular. But there was a hell of a lot more to him than looks. Wild Bill had the greatest sharpshooter, knife throwing, ax welding act I've ever seen, and believe me, as long as I played the circuit, more than forty years, I've seen all the great ones including Sundown Slim and Texas Jack Murdock. Wild Bill performed tricks those bums wouldn't even dream about.

To the sound of the William Tell Overture, he would rush on stage dressed in a western outfit full of fringe and topped with a wide-brim Stetson. He paraded around in hand tooled-leather boots decorated in reds and greens mixed with brown. But the most impressive part of his dress was strapped to his waist, twin pearl-handled .45's, the polished metal reflecting light like mirrors. "The real McCoy," he told me once in reference to the weapons. "Owned by John Westley Hardin, the most feared killer in the Old West. From what I've read, each of these .45's is responsible for the deaths of at least ten men. Killing machines they were, perfectly balanced, perfectly calibrated. They're works of art made by Smithers of Santa Fe. He was the greatest of all the frontier gunsmiths, better than Remington, better than Colt. Smithers tooled every single part and assembled each pistol by hand. He made less than a thousand, and I doubt fifty exist today. He was a master craftsman, a first rate artist, the best there ever was."

Wild Bill's act started slowly. His wife threw a tin can in the air, and he picked it off with ease. Then she threw two, and he blew holes in those, too. Then she tossed up three, and once more he took all three out of the air. He holstered his pistol, his wife grabbed another half dozen cans, and with one mighty heave, send them skyward. His left hand a blur, the pistol barked-- onetwothreefourfivesix--just like that, faster than you could say the words. I never saw him miss, not once.

Every other fast draw act I knew used buckshot in their loads, but not Wild Bill. At one point in his act, his wife lighted a cigarette and stood sideways, her profile to Wild Bill. Using his right hand, he drew his pistol and fired from behind his back, cutting the cigarette in half. That never failed to draw gasps from the audiences, but then he shifted his position and did the same with the other hand. If he used buckshot, he would have blown away half her face.

"I could never use buckshot," he told me. "That would be cheating. I spent my whole life making sure I was the best there is, and I'm going to give my fans the real thing every time I go out there on the stage."

"Some of them are going to think you're a fake no matter what you do," I said.

He shrugged. "I can't help what they think. But the day I have to resort to tricks to fool people, that's the day I quit."

His act, as all good acts do, ended with the greatest feat of all. He strapped his wife on a wheel and sent her spinning. True, the wheel was set at a fix speed that never varied, but that didn't make his feat any less exciting or any less real. On a table, lay five knives and five hand axes. With lightening speed, he swept up one knife after another and hurled them at the spinning wheel, then followed with the axes. When the wheel stopped, Marie was outlined by the weapons. I must have seen Will Bill do that trick a hundred times, and I swear he hit the same exact marks every time.

Except after one performance, I found him before the empty spinning wheel tossing the knives and axes in a fevered haste. I had never seen him practice between shows. I waited until he tossed the last blade before I asked "What the hell you doing, Bill?"

"During the last show, I was off a good quarter of an inch to the right on one of my throws," he said. "I knew the moment I let it go."

"A quarter of an inch!" I laughed. "That's downright terrible. You ought to give it up right now and go back to selling Bibles."

"It's not funny." His face was pinched with concern. "My act depends on perfection--absolute perfection. Anything less isn't acceptable."

"Nobody's perfect," I said.

"I have to be."

So that was Wild Bill. He and Marie had been with Warbling Brothers Road Show and Circus close to five years, and outside the hoochie kooch, he was the biggest draw among the side tops. In those days western movies were big draws and John Wayne and Gary Cooper national heroes. People still attended rodeos, and you could hear The Lone Ranger on the radio. Hopalong Cassidy and Roy Rogers performed in their own Wild West shows, and kids idolized them.

Since we toured mainly small backwater towns in California, Arizona and Nevada, Wild Bill was made to order for those cowboys and ranchers who, day in and day out, made up the bulk of our attendance. He was at the top of his world, the best there ever was, playing to enthusiastic crowds who applauded his skills. Things couldn't get any better for him.

Then Cheryl Kipinski showed up. She was the cheesecake portion of Merlin the Magician's act, the pretty girl who distracts while the trickster fools his audience. They hired on in late June of '48, and right away she set her sights on Wild Bill. Now Marie, Bill's wife, wasn't a bad sort, although she nagged him more than necessary, and truth be told, she was a bit unkempt except when she was in costume on stage, but she could have dressed to the nines and covered herself in jewels and furs, and still, she could never match Cheryl in looks or figure. Or youth, since she was Marie's junior by ten years. Warbling Brothers Road Show and Circus hired a passel of good-looking women for one act or another, a couple I classified as beautiful, but Cheryl was the best of the best, the proverbial blonde bombshell, which also contrasted to the darker, more introspective Marie. I suspect just about every guy working for Warbling Brothers fantasized jumping in bed with Cheryl Kipinski, that is every guy except Merlin who was queer as a three dollar bill.

I'm unclear how the affair started. I don't even know

who made the first move, but I suspect Cheryl. Until she showed, Wild Bill's only real passion in life seemed to lie in perfecting his already perfect art. If he took notice of any female other than his wife, I never saw it. But Cheryl, dressed in her skimpy costume showing a lot of breast and thigh, managed to catch him between shows, and working her wiles, reeled him in.

And that poor bastard fell as hard as a guy can. Whenever Cheryl came near, he couldn't take his eyes off her, and he got this pained expression like he was having a bad gas attack. Later, when he wasn't on stage, he would disappear for long stretches, and no one would see him or Cheryl. By that time, we all knew what they were up to. Maybe Marie knew, too, but if she did, she never let on.

One night Wild Bill and Cheryl snuck off to a motel, and after expending themselves in lovemaking, lay in bed clinging to each other. That's when Cheryl first broached the subject, although indirectly. She buried her head in his shoulder. "Why what's wrong, honey?" Wild Bill asked her.

"I hate this sneaking around. Oh Bill, I want to be with you all the time."

"Me, too, Honey. Me, too."

That was the night he began to see Cheryl in his wife's place, not only as his wife but also as his partner on the stage. What an attraction, he the world's greatest sharpshooter, knife thrower, ax welder, she with her movie star looks. Warbling Brothers Road Show and Circus wouldn't be able to contain them. They would have to find a bigger venue, maybe even set up their own Wild West show, tour the country, tour the world, meet with royalty, hobnob with princes and kings, all the while making a goddamned fortune.

There was only one drawback. His wife owned the rights to half of the act. If he left her, he would have to give up the Wild Bill Saunders persona and start over. Sure, he knew people in the business, and they could book him engagements, but it would be a long climb back to the top.

The next time he and Cheryl slipped off together, he explained the problems of leaving his wife. Cheryl cried, and Bill hated it when a woman cried. He didn't know how he was supposed to act. "I'll figure something out," he said. "Stop crying now. I promise I'll take care of it."

"She's the only thing standing in the way of our happiness," Cheryl said between sobs.

Those words, so calculating in their meaning, planted the seed in Bill's mind that only Marie's death would free him. With her out of the way, the act was his and his alone, and he and Cheryl could be together. But how to accomplish it without getting caught? Every time he drew up a plan, he weighed the probability of success against spending the rest of his life in jail.

It was Cheryl who hit upon not only a sensible but also a foolproof plan. One hot night in Barstow, he and Cheryl crept off between acts, and hidden deep in shadows behind the trucks, she explained. "You kill her right on stage during the act. Just a little shift of your hand, and you can put a bullet through her head or a knife in her heart. You could claim it was an accident, and you'd have all those witnesses to back you up. Oh darling, don't you see? It's perfect. You'll do it, won't you, darling? You'll do it for us?"

He stiffened. "I don't know--I--" She began to cry, the tears rolling down her face and streaking her mascara and rouge. "Yeah, sure," he said. "During the act."

"When?" she asked. "Tonight? Tomorrow?"

"Soon," he said.

But that night when Wild Bill performed his act, it went off as usual. He shot the cigarettes out of Marie's mouth and outlined her with the knives and axes. And the same results followed the next two nights. When Cheryl and Wild Bill once more found their way to a motel, she discovered his ardor cooled. "What's bothering you, darling? You're still going through with it, aren't you? You still love me, don't you?"

"Sure," he said, but his voice lacked enthusiasm.

She began to cry, and he held her tighter so he didn't have to look in her eyes. "I'm just trying to see all the angles. Give me a couple more days, and I'll settle things."

Those couple of days passed and then a couple of more. Soon it was a week later, than a month, and still Will Bill had not killed his wife. During that month, Cheryl and Bill saw each other only in passing, and Bill refused to look at her as if she wasn't there. At first Cheryl thought this might be part of the plan, as a way to avert suspicion, but after a while his coldness struck her as far more than that. So one night after his last performance, she caught him walking back to his trailer and pulled him off into the shadows.

By that time, they were back in Lompoc where it all began. A cold wind blew in off the Pacific, less than a mile from town, so close that in the still of the night they could hear waves beat against the shore. "What's going on, Bill? I thought you loved me. I thought you wanted to be with me." She began to cry softly, dabbing her eyes with a handkerchief. This tactic had always worked before with Bill, it would work again. She stepped in close, pressing her body against his. "Why haven't you done what we agreed on? If you really loved me, you would've done it by now."

With both hands on her shoulders, he held her at arms' length, his only answer a shake of his head, and she saw then her tears were useless. "You were never going to do it, were you? You were just stringing me along to have your way with me."

"That's not it," he said, and she heard a resolve in his voice she had not heard before.

"You don't love me." She spit the words at him. "You just wanted in my pants like every other son-of-a-bitch I've ever known."

He dropped his hands to his side, his shoulders slumping. "You can think that, but it's not true. I made up my mind to kill Marie. I had it all planned out. I just couldn't do it."

"Your conscience got in the way." Her tone sounded angry and cynical.

"Conscience didn't have anything to do with it," he said.

"Then you're a damn coward."
"That may be, but it's still not the reason."
"Then what is?"
"I don't know if you'll understand."
"Just try me," she said.

He leaned against the cab of an empty truck, his arms folded across his chest. "I can betray my wife. That's easy enough. I've already done that. I can betray my friends and family. Hell, if I had kids, I guess I could betray them. But my act--that's me, that's all I've got. I betray it, I betray myself, and no man should ever do that." When she didn't answer right away, he said, "See. I knew you wouldn't understand." He pushed himself from the truck and began to walk away.

"I'll tell your wife!" she screamed at his back. "I'll tell her all about us. What'll happen to your precious act then?"

He never looked back and said, "I've already told her."

Not much left to the story. Wild Bill and Marie continued their act as if nothing happened, and Bill even added a few extra tricks like throwing three quarters into the air simultaneously and plugging each dead center before they hit the ground. Then he gave each of the dented quarters to a kid in the audience. It was the addition of that trick that landed Will Bill a contract with Ringling Brothers with a guaranteed forty grand a year, a huge sum at that time for a circus act.

As for Cheryl, she persuaded Merlin that, if he didn't marry her, she would leave him. They lasted three years with Warbling Brothers before arthritis killed his act, and during that time, Cheryl screwed anybody with pants, but as far as I know, she never again tried to steal another woman's husband. Of course by then, we were all on to her.

Two or three years after she left the show, I ran into her in Lompoc of all places. After the show closed one night, I went into town to get a beer, and there she was sitting at the bar nursing a drink. When I sat on the stool next to her, she recognized me right away. Her face was bloated, and she carried an extra twenty pounds. Don't get me wrong. She was still an attractive woman, but booze had destroyed that breathtaking beauty she once possessed.

We exchanged 'hellos,' and I asked about Merlin.

She laughed. "I drove the little bugger into the arms of another man." We talked a while longer, and she asked about various people we knew, but she was a drunk, and almost as soon as I sat down, I wanted to be away from her. Still, I made myself finish my beer before I tossed a dollar on the counter and tried to make my escape. "You ever hear from Wild Bill?" she asked.

I started to lie, to tell her I had no idea where he was, but I thought: What the hell can she do now? "He's in France. They love him over there. He's started his own Wild West show and touring Europe."

"Good for him." She held her drink aloft as she stared at herself in the mirror behind the bar. "Here's to Wild Bill, a real artist. The best there ever was."

CHAPTER SEVENTEEN

Waco: A Comedy in Four Acts

1.

Once upon a time, my mother Giselle, joined Warbling Brothers Road Show and Circus. The man who loved her in the wrong way was my father, Roger Medavoy, a small time crook in the employment of Bugsy Siegel. And the man who set things right, we knew only as Waco.

My mother first met Roger on a Friday afternoon at Schwab's Drugstore where legend says a producer discovered Lana Turner. Girls were always going there hoping to be discovered, and Giselle Florey was no different from hundreds of other hopefuls, a pretty girl, prettier than Lana Turner, blonde, blue-eyed, a Southern California natural. She could sing and dance and act, a star waiting to be discovered. Everyday after Hollywood High let out--she was a junior in that year of 1945--she wandered down the Strip to Swchwab's, sat at the counter and ordered a vanilla Coke. She always brought a book from the library, usually a Bronte or an Austin, and she would sit for an hour reading, but whenever a man dressed in a suit entered, she would look up and see if he noticed her. Plenty noticed, but if any was a producer or agent, he never made it known.

On the other hand, servicemen were always coming in. The war in Japan had ended a scant month before, and Navy men were especially prominent. Plenty of those noticed her, too, and once in a while, one got up enough nerve to approach, but she discouraged them by refusing to take her nose out of the book. Then in walked Roger Medavoy, still in his uniform but already running errands for Bugsy Siegel. When he sat on the stool next to her, she kept her eyes on JANE EYRE, which she was reading for the third time. He said, "Now that's a real good book. Yessir, real good." In reality, Roger had never read the book--he only read comics and sports in the newspaper--but he knew how to start a conversation with a pretty girl. And he had seen the movie, at least the first half hour or so until he had fallen asleep.

She lifted her eyes and discovered a sailor who looked surprisingly like Tyrone Power, especially the dark eyebrows and penetrating eyes.

"You've read it?" Her question sounded more shocked than disbelieving.

"Sure thing," he said.

"I've never known one boy who read *Jane Eyre*. Not one." She closed the book but kept her finger to mark the page where she left off. "You really liked it? Really?"

"Can't think of one I liked better," he said.

"What part did you like the best?" She sipped the vanilla Coke, her eyes glued to his face. He sensed the question was not a test--she didn't appear the least bit suspicious of his motives--but rather she honestly wanted to know.

"The scenes in the orphanage." Since these were the only scenes from the film he remembered, it was his only answer. He added, "Pretty strong stuff."

"But what about Jane and Rodchester? I mean, don't you think their love was--oh--just too much to bear?" One hand rose to her throat like a woman on the verge of the vapors.

"Sure, absolutely. But I grew up in an orphanage. So that early stuff hit pretty hard, see."

On this particular point, Roger told the truth. From the time he was an infant until he turned seventeen--with a couple of short stints in foster homes--he was a ward of the Odd Fellows Home for Orphaned Boys in Bakersfield. Ordinarily the home kept boys until they were eighteen, but because of his many scrapes and troubles, especially with other wards of the institution, the Board of Trustees fudged on his paperwork. Two of the keepers--substitute the word 'guards,' for 'keepers', if you will--packed his belongings into one small canvas bag, shoved five dollars in his pocket, and escorted him to the gate, to be met there by the supervisor, Mr. Lamont Jordon, who told Roger that if he ever again showed his face around the home, the police would arrest him and throw his butt in jail. This was after he had beaten one kid so badly he almost died and extorted money and favors from a dozen others too weak or scared to protest.

Ordinarily my father didn't talk about those days, but here he sensed an advantage, which he wasn't above using. "Let me tell you, the people who ran my orphanage make the ones in this--" With his index finger, he tapped the book my mother held. "--look like cream puffs. They worked us like slaves. They had us out in the corn fields hoeing and planting all day. Some of the kids were only eight or nine. All we got for supper was soup and a piece of bread. When we were lucky, we got a bite of meat in our soup."

"How terrible!" my mother said. "How dreadful!"

"Don't get me wrong. It toughened me up--" He tapped the novel again. "--just like it toughened up the girl, this Jane Erie. That's why I liked the book, see. This girl--me and her are a lot alike. I understand her, see."

He had a way of occasionally ending his sentences with 'see,' like he was playing at being Jimmy Cagney, but my mother, rather than finding it intimidating, thought it cute and endearing.

He glanced at his watch, and said, "Look, it's getting close to five, and I haven't had a bite to eat all day. I've been running errands for this friend of mine."

"Errands for a friend?" my mother said. "I thought you were in the navy."

"Just waiting on my discharge papers." He smiled and tapped his chest. "Listen, you're talking to a real life hero, see. I was on the *Indianapolis*. Ever here of it?"

"You dropped the atomic bomb?"

He shook his head. "No, no, I was on the ship that carried the plane that dropped the bomb. We sent the plane on its way, and then On July 30th--I'll remember that day like it was my birthday--we were torpedoed, and the ship went down. I was all alone on a raft for six days out in the middle of the ocean, just me and sharks, until a rescue plane spotted me. So I'm a hero, see."

In this Roger also told the truth, at least to a degree. He was indeed a survivor of the *Indianapolis*, he was on a lifeboat for six days, and he was alone when the rescue plane swept down and carried him away. However, an odd fact emerges when one investigates the circumstances. Of the more than three hundred survivors rescued from the *Indianapolis*, only a handful managed to get to lifeboats. In most cases, boats were so overloaded, men were in the water clinging to the gunwales. Yet Roger was alone, and when they found him, and appeared, except for a bad sunburn, no worse for wear. He still had food and water for another week. Make of that what you will.

At the time, my mother knew only what Roger told her, which she accepted at face value. And of course, he looked so handsome in his uniform. All of this, and he knew *Jane Eyre*, even if he did pronounce her name incorrectly. When he asked her to have dinner with him, she felt she couldn't refuse. After all, he was a hero who had helped to end the war.

She thought of calling home to tell her parents, but her father, a believer in Old Testament retribution and damnation, would have ordered her home. He was an unforgiving, rigid man who ranted against her desire to be a star, calling movies "satan's temptation." Whenever she went to a film with one of her friends, she kept it to herself. On the other hand, her mother, quiet as a church mouse, constantly gave in to her more bombastic husband.

So my mother, Giselle, said yes, she would love to have dinner with him, and Roger Medavoy told her to wait a moment, he had to see a man about a debt. He took himself off to the back of the drug store where he found the manager, a burly man with a gambling addition. Giselle heard a body crash into shelves and bottles and boxes hit the floor. A moment later Roger reappeared. Smiling, he said, "A guy back there slipped on the wet floor. Kind of funny, don't you think? I mean, here we are in a drugstore, and a guy almost gets himself killed."

"It's ironic," she said.

His brows narrowed as if he were trying to discern some hidden meaning in her comment, but she met his gaze with wide eyed-innocence. "Yeah, sure," he said, and taking her arm, helped her off the stool. "Come on, let's get out of here. I'd hate for one of us to take a spill."

He had a car parked just outside, a big Oldsmobile built before the war but in perfect shape, its deep black finish polished so that it reflected images like a mirror. The Olds belonged to Bugsy Siegel, but my mother didn't know that either, or, I suspect, did she care. She had never heard of the gangster.

She had no idea where Roger was taking her until he pulled up in front of Ciro's on the Strip, and a young boy, only a year or two older than she, opened her door. Sliding out, she pulled at her dress to keep it from riding up her legs. Still in her school clothes, she felt woefully underdressed and out of place. Ciro's! My god, she had heard of this place all her life, she had seen it in movie magazines and newspapers, and once with her mother, she had ridden past on a bus on the way to a doctor's appointment, but she had never really seen it, not like this, up close. Of course in her dreams she had seen herself here many times, a star surrounded by adoring fans, signing autographs, escorted by Clark Gable or Errol Flynn or--or Tyrone Power. Her heart beat faster, and she found it difficult to breathe.

Once inside, the Maître d' escorted them to a table in the rear, potted plants on each side, which made it feel isolated and apart from the rest of the restaurant, yet when she sat, she could view the whole interior. She caught her breath, holding it in disbelief, for there, just two tables away sat Frank Sinatra and his wife Nancy, favorites of the movie magazines. The piano player began a rendition of "The House I Live In," the crooner's current hit. Roger waved, Sinatra saw and offered a salute in return.

"You know Sinatra?" my mother asked.

"I met him a few times," he said. "Ben Siegel introduced us."

When the waiter came, my father ordered a bottle of Champaign and two glasses. With a raised brow, the waiter glanced at my mother, but said nothing and hurried to fill the order. "I don't drink," my mother said.

"Just one glass." Roger reached across the table and took my mother's hand. "To celebrate us getting to know each other, see."

So my mother had her first drink, which made her slightly giddy, but to her credit, she refused a second, and Roger didn't push her. He ordered dinner, lobster for both. She had never eaten lobster either, and when it arrived, the meat sticking out of the tail, she feared she might not like it. After all, she hated fish. Following Roger's actions, she dipped a small piece in butter, slipped it between her lips, and discovered, much to her amazement, she liked it. No, 'like' was too weak a word. She loved it.

When they finished dinner and the waiter came again, Roger pulled out a roll of bills, peeled off a twenty, and flipped it on the table. By the time they left Ciro's, my mother was completely taken in, her head in the proverbial clouds, but when Roger suggested they go back to his place for a little music and dancing, she had the good sense to say she needed to get home, that her parents would already be furious. She asked Roger to park a block away from the house, and under a pepper tree thick with foliage, she allowed him to kiss her, but when his hand crept toward her breast, she pushed him away and jumped out of the car, her face flushed, the wine and the evening almost too much to bear. Through the open car window, Roger said, "I'll see you tomorrow at the drugstore, same time. You be there, you hear? I'm going to be real disappointed if you're not. I might even have to come looking for you."

He drove off, the Olds roaring like a wounded lion, his headlights cutting a path through the dark night. She waited a few minutes trying to settle her nerves and waiting for the sound of the car to fade. She didn't want her father to connect the car with her coming home at such a late hour--she figured it was already well past eight, fast approaching nine--an unheard time for her to stay out on a school night. Even on the weekends her father imposed a ten pm curfew. In her head she had invented a story about doing homework with a school friend and loosing sight of the time.

They had kept the porch light on, and when she walked through the door, she discovered her parents seated on either side of the large radio listening to 'Mr. Keen, Tracer of Lost Persons.' Her father stood, his face red with anger. In his hands, he held a folded belt, snapping it twice, each time the crack as loud as a firecracker.

2.

They met the next day, and right away she went to his car and they drove to Hansen Dam, parking under a weeping willow in sight of the spillway, dry in the fall heat. "You've got to get me home before dark," my mother said.

"And why's that?" Roger asked.

My mother reached up and slipped the blouse from her shoulder, exposing a thick, red welt.

"What the hell—"

She slipped the blouse back into place. "My father."

"That son-of-a-bitch! Why, I ought to--" Roger struck his fist into the palm of his other hand. "You tell me it's all right, I'll do it, see. I'll give your old man the beating of his life."

They stayed there for more than half an hour, kissing and talking, talking and kissing, and twice he made moves on her, one hand inching toward a breast, and each time she grabbed his wrist and pulled it away. Just past four, she persuaded him to take her home. Twenty minutes later, he once more parked a block from her house. By this time the sun hung just above the western mountains, casting long shadows that stretched from one side of the street to the other. She kissed him once, their lips barely touching, before she was out of the car and heading up the street. He waited by the curb, the motor idling, and watched until she disappeared into a house.

Afterward he collected a couple of debts for Siegel, disappointed that neither of the suckers offered the least bit of resistance. He drove over to a five and dime hotel on Santa Monica where he delivered fifty-five dollars to Lew, one of Bugsy's bookkeepers. Upstairs was a whorehouse, and Roger climbed the stairs and spent the night with a girl from Siegel's stable. But he couldn't take his mind off my mother, her face haunting him like a ghost, so that whenever he looked at the whore, he saw my mother. Only the woman wasn't my mother, and afterward as he lay in bed smoking, the whore asleep beside him, he felt overwhelmingly dissatisfied. He had never experienced such a reaction. Even the cigarette tasted bitter, the smell stringent, and he crushed it in the ashtray on the nightstand.

He just couldn't shake the image of her face. Sure she was good-looking, but he had bedded plenty like her over the last few years. Girls were a dime a dozen for a guy with his looks, and picking them up and getting them into bed was a done deal the moment he made his move. So maybe this one had held him off for a couple of days, but in the end, he would have her just like all the others. So why did she bother him so? Dropping his head on the pillow, he flipped off the lamp and tried to sleep.

Just a few miles away, my mother sat at the kitchen table completing the last of her homework, a book report on *Jane Eyre*, and even as she put words to paper, she kept seeing the young sailor who had also read the book and who looked surprisingly like Tyrone Power. Occasionally she would recall their kisses, her finger caressing her lips, and she would stare at the icebox without seeing it.

Twice during the evening her father--my grandfather--came in the kitchen to glare at her with undisguised anger. He had told her to come home right after school, but she dragged herself in at sunset. By that time, her father was already home from Warner Brothers where he worked as a guard. She made excuses that she had to stay after school to work with the drama teacher who was planning to put her a play. Reluctantly he accepted it, although he reminded her of the belt by touching the buckle, drawing her attention to it. "You come home late tomorrow, you'll get it for sure," he told her. "No excuses."

She held tears back, not wanting to appear weak because then he might see her lies. If he found out about Roger, he would make sure the two of them never saw one another again. She wouldn't let that happen. But what was she to do?

Her father stood over her, an angry scrowl twisting his features. "I know you think I'm being hard on you, but I've seen the kind of evil the studios bring to this town. I know they can turn a young girl's head, fill it with all sorts of sinful thoughts." At this point, his voice softened, and he laid a beefy hand on her shoulder. "I don't do this to hurt you, but you're a child. You don't know the kind of trouble you can get yourself into."

She didn't hate him all the time. There were moments when she convinced herself she could love him-- should love him, for daughters were supposed to love their fathers. That particular delusion usually lasted only a few minutes. Then she would remember the last time he had taken a belt to her, which happened all too often, even for minor infractions. Her mother always sat silently by, never interfering, herself a recipient of puritanical punishments.

The next day, Roger picked her up at school and drove out to Hansen Dam where they parked under the same tree. A cold wind blew in from the north, and Roger kept the motor running, the heater blowing on their feet. They kissed often, their bodies pressed together, and the windows fogged over. When his hand again sought her breast, she allowed him the barest touch before she pulled away and broke their embrace. In this area at least, she heeded her father's warnings, and she would not let Roger have his way.

"Look, I ain't no kid, see. You can't keep doing this to me." Breathing heavily, he said, "Don't you like me? I'm not bad looking. I treat you all right, don't I?"

"Yes."

"What's the problem? You like me, I like you."

"What you want from me--that's for married people." She turned her head, staring at the fogged window. She felt like crying, but again she refused to give in to girlish emotions.

"Then we better get married," Roger said.

My mother continued to stare at the window, her breath adding another coat of fog. Roger reached across the seat and pulled my mother to him. "Come on, give me a kiss. At least we can do that for now."

That evening, my mother packed a small bag with extra clothes and cosmetics, and stealing out after her parents had gone to bed, stashed it under a hedge by the front door. When her alarm clock rang at five-thirty, she leapt out of bed and dressed quickly. She was half out the front door when she heard her parent's clock clanging away, and scampering down the porch, swept up her bag behind the bushes. Half a block down, Roger flashed his headlights, and she ran to meet him.

They drove for over six hours until they crossed the border into Nevada, stopping at Roach, the first town they came to. In reality, it wasn't so much a town as a rest stop complete with a hotel / saloon, a filling station and a wedding chapel. In Nevada, you didn't need a wedding license, and the legal age to marry without parental permission was seventeen. My mother had turned that exalted age a month before in September.

Roger parked the Olds before the Forever Wedding Chapel. He still wore his navy uniform, although the day before he had received his discharge papers. Clutching my mother around the waist, he led her inside. The one room chapel lay in heavy shadows, the slightly raised altar decorated with an carved arch so old the varnish had rubbed off in spots. Fake flowers in large vases set on both sides of the arch, all of it covered in a fine layer of dust.

The Justice of the Peace who looked a great deal like Peter Lorre, his eyes round and bulging, read the wedding vows in a monotone so low Roger and my mother had trouble hearing. His rotund wife acted as witness. The ceremony from first word to last took all of three minutes, after which Roger paid the requisite ten dollars. My mother left the chapel with a small bouquet plus a gold band Roger purchased from the couple for an additional forty-five dollars.

Hurrying next door, they entered the Last Chance Saloon and Hotel, renting a room over the gambling hall where all night they heard the slot machines so clearly they sounded as if they were in the room with them. My mother never divulged the intimate facts surrounding that day and night they spent in the room--nor do I have any desire to know--except she once told me that Roger attempted to be gentle, but because of the type of women he had known, gentle was not part of the repertoire. He proved clumsy and forceful.

Once during their infrequent pauses, she took herself off to the bathroom, and returning, passed the dresser where, in a frenzy of undressing, Roger had emptied his pockets: a bulky wallet, a comb with broken strands of hair curled around the teeth, a handful of coins and a pair of brass knuckles. This last item, reflecting dying sunlight, caught her attention, and she stopped to inspect them. Lifting them between a forefinger and thumb, she held them aloft. "What's this for?"

He lay in bed, his hands propped behind his head, studying her with sleepy, indolent eyes. "They come in handy in my line of work."

Right then she began to wonder who she had married. After all, what did she know of this man, her senior by ten years? She had been blinded by his good looks and his stories about the war. He must have seen the momentary doubt in her eyes, and he said, "I'm a bill collector."

She said, "But sometimes people don't have the money to pay their bills."

He laughed. "With me, they pay, one way or another." It wasn't until their second week together that he slapped her for the first time. They had moved into The Crescent Arms, a block off Hollywood and Highland. Each day, even on the weekends, he was off collecting debts and running errands, leaving her alone most of the time. On a Thursday, he came home early, his lip cracked and bleeding and found her reading *Jane Eyre* again. He knocked the book from her hands and raked his knuckles across her face. She cried, and he promised never to do it again.

For a long time, he kept his word, until the day she told him she was pregnant, and cursing, he slammed his fist into her jaw, splitting her lip and knocking her to the floor. He picked her up, laid her on the bed and said he was sorry, that the news was so unexpected it shocked him. He swore on his mother's life he would never hit her again. She would just need to get a little operation, and then everything would be fine. After a couple of phone calls, he announced that Monday morning they had appointment in Tijuana. "Don't worry," he told her. "It's quick, and you won't feel much. We'll be back at it just a couple of days."

On Friday morning while Roger was out attending to business, she packed her one suitcase and went looking for any money that might be lying around the apartment. As she searched through his coats and pockets, she knocked loose a shoebox from the top shelf of the closet, and stacks on bills wrapped in rubber bands cascaded across the floor. By the time she gathered the bills and poured them on the bed, she had over three thousand dollars. She stuffed that in her suitcase, too, holding back a couple of twenties she slipped into her purse.

She left the Crescent Arms and caught a cab to Union Station where she boarded the Pacific Coast Special to San Francisco, the only passenger train of the day. All this time she feared Roger might return and find her gone. He would have no trouble tracking her. It was either the train or the bus. She didn't know what would happen if he did find her, except that it would be bad. She only began to feel safe when, just past ten in the morning, the train lurched forward and began to roll out of the station.

And so, in this way, my mother saved my life.

3.

At the Oakland train station, my mother purchased another ticket, this one for Denver, making a fuss at the window by pretending that she was about to throw up so the man behind the grate would remember her. She was planting a false trail. Later, she caught a local bus that ran to Berkeley, transferred to another and another. Just before ten that evening, she stood in the middle of the downtown Salsalito.

Across the street a filling station was in the process of closing, and with suitcase in hand, she walked over to the attendant and asked if he knew where she could rent a room. He directed her down the street to the Bayview Apartments. Her head lowered against the cold wind, she walked two blocks down the dimly lit street, shadows closing around her like a shroud.

From the outside, the Bayview Apartments, an old structure build in the twenties, appeared in need of a fresh coat of paint. A few lights were on downstairs, giving her hope, and she stepped on the porch, the wood groaning as if her small body was simply too much to bear. The window of a downstairs room was half open, light penetrating the lace curtains. From inside a woman's voice said, "Who's there?"

"A man down the street said you might have a room for rent."

The porch light came on, a door opened, and a thin woman in a housecoat stood peering out from behind a screen, her finger busily pushing at strains of hair that had come loose from the tight bun. "It's late to come looking for a room."

"The bus just let me off." A sudden surge of panic shook my mother. "You do have a room, don't you? Please say you have a room."

My mother's voice was so full of fear and doubt that the landlady, Mrs. Frankel, took pity on her. "I've got a room if you got the money."

Mrs. Frankel led my mother up a flight of stairs, and when she saw the small flat, the one window providing a view of San Francisco and the Bay, she paid a month's advance on the spot. As for the room, it wasn't much--a table, a couple of chairs, a sink and a stove. Mrs. Frankel took the two tens, stuffing the bills in her apron pocket. As she turned to leave, my mother said, "Where's the bed?"

Looking back over her shoulder, the landlady said, "Oh dear, you really are a little lamb, aren't you?" She pointed to a door that my mother had mistaken for the bathroom. "It's a fold down. Bath and toilet are down the hall. You share it with the other tenant on this floor."

"Other tenant?"

"That would be Waco. He works for a circus, and whenever they're in winter quarters, he lodges with me. But don't worry you're pretty little head. He's older than God, and I suspect he has no interest in young ladies. But, if you have any trouble, you come and get me." With that, Mrs. Frankel shuffled out, closing the door as she left.

My mother unpacked her suitcase, which filled only one drawer of the dresser. At that point, her long day's journey caught up with her, and suddenly exhausted, she dropped in a rocker beside the window, staring at San Francisco, the lights of the city reflected in the bay. She laid her head against the hard rim of the chair and closed her eyes, not intending to sleep, but she was dreaming within seconds.

Around five in the morning, the pressure from her bladder woke her. Outside a wall of white had descended, and she could barely see the street light in front of the house. Surprisingly the fog gave her a sense of safety, as if it were a wall behind which she hid.

Stiff and sore, she staggered down the hallway to the bathroom, the door open, the hall light on, showing her the way. The toilet seat was cracked in three places, and afterward she washed her hands in a sink stained brown with age. As she dried her hands, she felt a wave of weakness that almost buckled her knees, and she grabbed the towel rack for support. Swaying, she opened door, stepped into the hallway, and stumbled into the wall.

The door to the other apartment opened and an elderly man stepped out, most of his wrinkled face covered by a white beard. "What's wrong, Miss?" he asked.

"It's nothing." She tried to smile, but even that proved difficult. "I'm just--I'm--a little dizzy."

He came and took her by the arm. "Let me help you."

His grip was strong for such an old man, and she leaned into him as he guided her back to her room. She sat on the edge of the bed, her head lowered, as she waited for the world to stop spinning. "When's the last time you ate?" he asked.

Of course--that was the problem. More than thirty hours had passed since her last meal, and at that moment, her stomach grumbled. The old man said, "I'll be right back."

He returned, offering her what appeared to be a piece of leather. "This is jerky. You know what jerky is?" She shook her head, and he said, "It's dried beef. The juice will give you strength."

She took the jerky. "You're Mr. Waco."

"Don't deserve no 'mister.' Just Waco."

It took all her strength to chew the tough strip of meat, but immediately she began to feel the heaviness leave her arms and legs.

"How long have you been in family way?" he asked.

Surprised, she looked up. "You can tell?"

"I'm old. I ain't blind." He pointed to her left hand. "I can see the ring. I suppose your husband gave you that busted lip."

She knew she should be reticent about answering--people who knew too much could betray her--yet she needed to talk, say it out loud, have someone hear. "He hit me only twice. Maybe I would've stayed--" Her hand caressed her belly. "--but he wanted me to do something so terrible--"

"Did you go to the police?"

"Roger works for some very bad people. There's this man named Siegel--"

"Bugsy Siegel?"

"You know him?"

"Heard of him. Never met him."

"If I had gone to the police—"

"You're right. It wouldn't have done any good."

She began to cry, not hysterical sobbing or anything like that, but tears rolling free, spotting her blouse. It was the first time she had allowed herself to cry in over four years. "If Roger finds me--"

"We have to make sure that doesn't happen." Waco smiled for the first time, showing a set of blindingly white teeth.

"You go back to bed, darlin'. Get some rest, and when you wake up, we'll get you a proper breakfast. Millie's is just up the street, and she makes the best biscuits and gravy you ever ate." He walked to the door where he paused. "You're safe here. You have my word."

"I'm sorry for disturbing you so early in the morning," my mother said.

"Hell, darlin', I don't sleep much any more. Got no time for it." He closed the door and left her alone. Just before she drifted off, she heard outside her door a chair scrape the floor and a body settle in.

Over the next few months, my mother seldom left the apartment, and when she did, she went down the road to the grocery store or up the road to the drug store. From a second hand shop she bought a dozen books that kept her reading late into the nights. Now you might think she lived a boring existence during this time as she grew bigger with me, but in this you would be wrong. Waco was there, and he taught her to play checkers, and when she finally got so good that she beat him with regularity, he taught her chess.

And all the time he regaled her with his stories.

As a young man, he had ridden with the great trail herds from Texas to Kansas, and he told her of meeting such luminaries as Wyatt Earp and Bat Masterson, Clay Allison and Doc Halliday. "Earp was a ruthless bastard." He parted his white hair and showed her an old scar. "He buffaloed me with his .45. Split me open like I was a melon. I had a headache for a month."

"Why did he do that?"

He scratched his beard, small flakes of dry skin floating away. "Me and this other waddie got into an argument--over a girl. It came to gunplay. So he arrested me."

Suddenly serious, my mother said, "You killed a man?"

"I could have. I was pretty fast in those days." He shook his head. "Naw, I put a bullet in his shoulder. Hell, he was a friend of mine. I didn't want to hurt him bad."

"Your friend? But you shot him."

"The son-of-a-bitch was going to shoot me." He grinned. "It was different in them days. We was all a little wild."

Because he looked so comical with his hair and beard sticking out all directions, she had trouble seeing him as a dangerous gunman, so as a result, she put many of his stories down to exaggeration. Still, she came to love this old man. He took care of her, better than anyone ever had. He made sure she ate right, he got her whatever she needed, and he promised when her time came he would be there with her. "Hell, darlin', you're too young to be all by yourself," he told her. "I'm just sorry it has to be an old codger like me."

In her sixth month, he took her to a doctor for the first time. "Just making sure everything is all right," he said. The doctor asked questions and listened to our hearts, at the end of which he pronounced us both healthy. He wrote a prescription for vitamins and told her to come back in a month.

As they left the office, my mother said, "I told you I was fine."

"In my day, women lost children by the wagonloads," Waco said. "My own mama had ten kids. Only three lived past five."

"When was the last time you saw a doctor?" my mother asked.

He thought a moment, trying to recall. "I guess it was '88 0r '89. A sawbones dug a couple of bullets out of me."

My mother laughed. "Another friendly shooting, I suppose."

His expression hardened. "I robbed a bank in Dalhart, Texas. It cost me two years in Huntsville." In almost a whisper, he added, "And it cost me a lot more than those two years."

Despite his confession, my mother felt safe with Waco. Her fears returned only when he went off to attend to his duties with Warbling Brothers Road Show and Circus, encamped just outside Richmond a few miles away. Every day for a couple of hours in the morning and a couple of hours in the evening, he would get in his truck and drive there and back. During those times, her anxiety returned the moment she heard the motor start up and lasted until she heard him return. To calm her fears, she would bury herself in a book, but the tension never left her shoulders and neck, so by the time Waco walked through the door, he would have to massage the affected areas until the muscles loosened and she could breathe easily again.

Then, in mid-March, the world changed. Waco announced that the show was about to go back on the road, and he would be leaving within a couple of days. By that time my mother was heavy with me. "An elephant on two beanpoles," she said of herself.

On the same day, while Waco was off doing his job, Mrs. Frankel came to my mother and told her a private detective was asking around town about Giselle Florey. "It won't be long before he knows you're here. Maybe he already knows." Mrs. Frankel must have seen the fear register in my mother's face, and she reached out and patted her hand. "If he comes, I'll tell him you stepped out for a while. We'll wait for Waco to get back. He'll know what to do."

My mother spent the next hour afraid that any moment the detective would come bursting into her room. Once she sidled up to the window, daring to peek through the thin lace curtains. Across the street, a round little man leaned against a telephone pole, his eyes glued to the house. He glanced up. She jumped back, fearing he had seen her. She ran to the closet, pulled out her suitcase and threw it on the bed. In a matter of minutes, she packed everything she owned except the books, most of which she had already read. The money she had taken from Roger--still over $2500--she stuffed in her purse. If Waco didn't return soon, she didn't know what she would do. He was the only one who could help her now.

But my mother did not know that the man across the street, an operative for the Continental Detective Agency, had already provided help. He had discovered my mother's whereabouts late the evening before, at which time he phoned Roger, who had that morning taken a plane out of LA, and who, at that very moment was on a ferry crossing the fog enshrouded Bay from San Francisco. But the detective discovered far more than Roger intended. When Roger hired the agency, he told them his wife was a thief who had stolen $5000 dollars and fled. Of course, the detective, being one of the best at his job, soon discovered the truth, and he didn't like Roger or the people Roger worked for. He couldn't warn the girl directly that her husband was on the way--that would violate his ethical code-- so that morning he went to every business in town announcing he was a detective looking for Giselle Florey, knowing without a doubt word would reach her.

For now, under a leaden sky, he kept his eye on the house. Once he saw the flutter of an upstairs curtain, and right then he knew she knew. He stood there another hour waiting for his client, hoping the girl would use the time to make her getaway, but the only activity he saw was the arrival of an old truck with a driver so grizzled he looked more reprobate than lodger. His jeans were covered in dirt and sawdust, his Stetson so battered it looked older than the man. The old man stayed in the house all of five minutes before he returned alone to his truck and drove away.

Ten minutes later, Roger Medavoy, gritting his teeth like he was constipated, came hurrying up the street from the ferry depot. He wore a dark suit, the coat showing a slight bulge under his left arm where he carried his piece. Without a word, the two men crossed the street. Mrs. Frankel met them on the porch, her arms folded across her chest, her face a stern mask. "If you men looking for a room, I've none available, and I thank you to get off my property."

Roger glanced at the pudgy detective. "Where is she?"

"She's got a room on the second floor."

"No one's home up there." Mrs. Frankel stepped in front of the screen door, blocking the stairs.

"Well?" Roger asked.

The detective shrugged. "I haven't seen her. Maybe she's there, maybe not."

Roger took a step toward Mrs. Frankel. "Get out of the way or so help me--" Mrs. Frankel held her ground, and Roger reached out, grabbed her arm and jerked her aside.

As he stepped past, Mrs. Frankel slugged him in the back of his head, her tiny fist cracking against bone. His eyes wild with anger, Roger turned on her. The little detective stepped between them. "Go see if your wife is home."

"When I come back--" Roger began.

"--we ain't doing nothing but leaving," the detective said.

Roger stomped up the stairs, his anger growing with each step. No one walked out on Roger Medavoy--no one—and he'd make sure she'd never do it again. He'd teach her a lesson she'd never forget. As for that bitch of a landlady--

Mrs. Frankel said to the detective, "She's not up there."
"Yes ma'am," he said, "I certainly hope you're right."

4.

My mother heard the footsteps on the stairs, and her whole body turned rigid with fear, not for herself but for me. In one last act of defiance, she snatched up the heavy glass ashtray on the nightstand, ready to bash in the skull of anyone who came through the door. From the landing, she heard the voice of Mrs. Frankel, and when the door opened, my mother faced Waco. Looking beyond her to the bed, he pointed to her suitcase. "Grab your things and go down the back stairs. Follow the alley up behind Millie's. I'll pick you up there."

She maneuvered the back stairs as best she could. I was due in a couple of weeks, and her belly stuck out so far it threatened her balance. She couldn't see the stairs directly in front, so she slid each foot carefully down before she took the next. Once she reached the bottom, she waddled down the unpaved alley trying to avoid the muddy ruts made by the garbage trucks. Bushes and fences covered her escape.

Waco stood beside the passenger's door, already open, the motor of his truck idling. He tossed her suitcase in the back, and taking her arm, steadied her while she climbed into the cab. By then, her breathing was ragged, her back radiated shape bolts of pain, and her heart beat with such ferocity it felt like it was trying to break free of her body. She began to fear the flight had brought on an early labor, but as Waco guided the truck out of town, her breathing returned to normal, the pain in her back subsided, and her heart settled into a steady rhythm. "Where are you taking me?" she asked.

"I've got that all figured out. You're joining me with Warbling Brothers Road Show and Circus." My mother started to protest that she knew nothing about circuses, but Waco, as if anticipating her objections, said, "I told them my granddaughter was moving in with me. I told them your husband run out on you, and you needed my help."

"You know, sooner or later, Roger will find me."

"I suspect so. We'll have to have the welcome mat ready."

Back at the Bayview apartments, Roger came stomping down the stairs, his anger boiling over, and when he saw Mrs. Frankel glaring at him, he threw back the flap of his coat and showed her the butt of his .38. "Tell me where she went or so help me--" He reached for his piece, ready to pistol whip the landlady into submission.

The little detective stepped between them, his hand on his own piece. "Like I said, we're leaving now."

Roger turned his black eyes on the rotund little man. "Get out of my way?"

The detective grunted. "You sure you want to pursue this disagreement? You're carrying a .38. I'm carrying a .45. Mine's bigger than yours."

Roger started to laugh until he realized the man wasn't joking--or bluffing. Already his hand rested on his weapon, and Roger had the distinct feeling the man wanted to use it. "You son-of—"

"Say it, and I'll kill you where you stand," said the detective.

Roger understood then he had grossly underestimated the detective. When the boss of the Continental Detective Agency said this was his best operative, Roger thought him nothing more than a trained bloodhound, but now he faced a man ready to pull down on him, one whose eyes were the coldest and most calculating he had even seen. Even Mickey Cohen, hard-eyed as he was, paled next to this man. "You're-- you're fired. And I'm not paying you one red cent. Not one--"

Roger stepped back trying to put distance between them, but the little man moved with him. "You're paying me right now. A hundred dollars a day for three days plus forty-three dollars for expenses." Roger's heel caught the porch railing, and he stopped abruptly, his backside pressed against the wood. "Shell out," the detective said, "or I'll shove my .45 so far down your throat it'll come out you ass." Without talking his eyes off Roger, he said, "Sorry, ma'am."

"That's quite all right," said Mrs. Frankel.

His hands shaking, Roger reached into his jacket and slowly brought out his wallet. The detective snatched the bills from his hand. He waved his thumb toward the street. "Now get off this lady's property."

Roger hurried out of the yard and up the street without looking back, his heels clicking against the pavement. Once the gangster turned the corner in the direction of the ferry terminal, the detective peeled off a twenty-dollar bill and handed it to the landlady. "This is for your trouble, ma'am. Sorry to have been such a bother."

Mrs. Frankel slipped the bill in her apron pocket. "You're a nice young man. You shouldn't associate with such riff raff."

"You don't meet many nice people in my occupation. Hazard of the job." He tipped his hat and stepped off the porch where he paused and looked at the overcast sky, the sun just beginning to break through. "Looks like it's going to be a nice day after all."

By five that afternoon, Waco had my mother safely stashed in his trailer, already loaded on a flatcar. Warbling Brothers had broken winter quarters and was on a train bound the next morning for Oxnard. As before, my mother worried that any minute Roger would come and find her, but after nightfall when he still hadn't shown, she relaxed enough to fall asleep in Waco's bed. While she slept, Waco sat by the front window, an old Colt single action .45 cradled in his lap. She awoke the next morning as the train lurched forward, and Waco was still there, the gun in his lap.

It was a week later in Oxnard my mother began her contractions, and Waco rushed her to the hospital where I was born April 1st, a day for fools. If I turn out to be such, I cannot blame my mother or Waco. They did the best they could for me.

Two months after I came into the world, Waco began to train my mother as a bareback rider. Her lithe, athletic figure made her a natural. For over two years my mother toured with Warbling Brothers, billed as Lily Divine. I have little recollection of those years, except to this day when I smell sawdust and sweat, my mind conjures up a picture of my mother astride a white charger as it circles the ring, a half dozen other horses following, an old man with a whip commanding his steeds.

Then in the spring of '48, Roger Medavoy found us once again, this time in Hemet, California, a desert community twenty-five miles west of Riverside. By that time, Bugsy Seigel was dead and Mickey Cohen was in charge of the rackets in

LA. Roger had not only survived the transition but moved up in the ranks from debt collector to enforcer. The cops attributed at least half a dozen gangland executions--perhaps even Bugsy himself--to Roger, but they had no proof, only suppositions.

I was barely two, full of baby fat and curiosity, the only child among the carny. Others had children, but they were older and gone from the nest or left behind with spouses or relatives, and because of that, I became a favorite of many, coddled and protected, seldom lacking for a companion or playmate, albeit a grownup one. I remember little of this, but my mother said it was so, and I trust her memory. My one memory is riding the white steed, holding to its mane and laughing, my mother behind holding me, the wind in my face, the hooves kicking up sawdust and dirt that burned my nose and stung my eyes.

During the shows, I stayed in my mother's dressing room, chaperoned by one of the acts that went on before or after my mother. At the end of every show, the entire ensemble of clowns, high wire acts, jugglers, and animal acts paraded around the tent to blaring music and applause. I was there, too, carried on the shoulders of one person or another.

It was at the beginning of April, a late Saturday night performance, that Roger watched from the bleachers, his gaze fixated on my mother, and he realized he had forgotten how beautiful she was. No, that wasn't it. She was more beautiful than he remembered. As he watched her maneuver the horse this way and that, controlling the beast with only the slightest pressure from her legs, he saw she was no longer the sixteen-year-old girl whom he married but a fully developed woman, slender and athletic, confident and desirable. Since she had run out on him three years before, he had slept with a hundred women, many who could satisfy a man's every sexual desire, and he had believed he no longer wanted her. All he wanted was revenge, but seeing her now, basking in the spotlight of fame and youth, he desired her more than ever.

At the end of the show, the troupe paraded out the rear of the tent, applause dying behind them. Waco lifted me off his shoulders, handing me to my mother. I stood beside her holding her hand, and as often happened, she talked with a couple of the performers before we headed to our trailer. She had no idea Roger lurked just off in the shadows, taking stock of her every move.

He waited until the crowd drifted away, then followed us to our trailer where my mother, nuzzling my neck and laughing, swing me up the stairs. Once inside, she reached back to close the door, and Roger caught it. When he stepped inside, she retreated, setting me on the floor, shielding me. He wore a silk suit, and a diamond ring sparkled on his left pinkie. The three years had wrought other changes as well. His face, grown puffy, especially around the eyes and mouth, reflected a life of indulgence and dissipation, and his once hard belly showed a small paunch. When he smiled, he exposed teeth stained faintly yellow.

She was still in her costume, her tanned legs exposed as well as the tops of her breasts, and his eyes devoured her. She felt naked under his gaze. "You didn't think you could hide from me forever, did you?" he said.

"Of course not. I'm surprised it took you this long."

With a casual nod in my direction, he said, "That my kid?"

"There's nothing here that belongs to you," my mother said. "And you'll be doing yourself a favor if you leave right now and never come back."

"You're my wife, he's my kid. You both belong to me."

"Just remember--I warned you." My mother spoke calmly and without fear.

That angered Roger. Ever since that detective had cowed him, he had worked hard to make people fear him, and he didn't like it one bit that this slip of a girl acted so cool and under control. He seized her arm, his fingers digging in the soft flesh above her elbow. "You're coming back to LA with me-- you and the kid."

"Like hell." She raked his cheek, drawing blood, and he slapped her, so hard it jarred her teeth. He slapped her a second time, letting go and sending her reeling to the floor where she landed half on top of me. I began to cry, and my mother sat up and took me in her arms, pressing my face into her shoulder.

Roger stepped forward, straddling us, his face flushed a crimson red. "You won't run away again, and you won't complain, and you'll do whatever I want. You know why? Because if you mess with me, something bad will happen to the kid, see." He flipped open his jacket, showing her the .38. "That's the way things are, see."

He reached again for my mother, and she spit in his face. He flinched, his anger exploding, and he drew back his hand, his fist closed, ready to smash her face.

He stiffened, his eyes widening in shock as a barrel of a pistol was jammed in his back. A voice said, "You move, and I'll put a hole in you I could ride a horse through." With his free hand, the man reached around and removed the piece from under Roger's jacket.

Still clutching me, my mother climbed to her feet. With the back of her hand she wiped blood from the corner of her mouth. "You poor, dumb bastard. I tried to warn you. We knew you'd come. We've been waiting for you."

Grabbing Roger by his coat collar, a hand hauled him to the door, and a kick to his backside sent him flying. He landed face down in the dust. Stunned, he lay unmoving until his head cleared, and he pushed himself to his hands and knees. Only then did he discover himself surrounded by more than a dozen men, performers still in their costumes and roustabouts in their working clothes. Each carried a hammer or a shovel or a pickax. Determined to show he wasn't afraid, he stood, his lips twisted into a snarl. "You guys don't know who you're messing with." He turned to the man who had so unceremoniously removed him from his wife's trailer and found a face and eyes as ancient as the desert itself. It was the man in the ring whose horses obeyed as if he spoke their language. He was still dressed in his western getup, the old Stetson, the jeans, the chaps, looking more like Gabby Hayes than Gabby Hayes. Roger would have laughed had the old man not held the Colt revolver cocked and pointed at his belly.

"This ain't over, old man." Roger wiped his mouth encrusted with dust. "I'll be back. You know I will."

"Mister, that was the wrong thing to say. Not that it matters any." The old man stepped down from the trailer and swung the pistol. The barrel cracked against Roger's skull.

Roger awoke to bright lights in his eyes. When he tried to sit up, blinding pain exploded in his head. He groaned.

A voice said, "'Bout time. You've been out over an hour."

Hands reached under his arms and hauled him to his feet. The man moved back in front of the lights, facing Roger, a good ten feet of open ground separating them. It was the old man from the circus--no one else was around--which gave Roger hope. After all, the old man must be eighty if a day. How dangerous could he be?

Roger forced himself to stand straight. Dust covered his jacket, and he slapped at the expensive silk, raising small clouds. He hoped the suit wasn't ruined. It had cost him a bundle. Quite calmly Roger said, "You know how many men I've killed, Gramps? You ain't got enough fingers on both hands to count that high. So if you know what's good for you--"

The old man chuckled. "Yeah, you're a real tough hombre. You're good at slapping around women and intimidating little boys. Hell, in my day, you wouldn't have lasted an hour. We would have would ripped out your liver and fed it to you. Maybe you're a big shot back in LA, but to me, you ain't nothing but a pissant."

"If I had my gun--" Roger began.

"It's under your arm, waiting for you." Waco tapped his hip. "I got mine, so when you're ready, make your move. I'll have plenty of time after you go for yourn."

Roger looked down, and sure enough, there was the .38 in his shoulder holster. "What the hell?" He lifted his eyes back to the old man, outlined by the lights from the truck. "You're crazy. This ain't the Old West."

"It is tonight."

Roger swallowed, his throat so full of dust his voice croaked like a frog's. "All those people back there--they saw me with you."

"They're family. No one's going to say anything. Anyway, you're free to go. All you got to do is get by me. That should be it easy for a tough guy like you."

Roger was sweating, and he tasted dust. "Do you know who I am?" Roger shouted.

"A dead man," said Waco.

Roger reached for his pistol.

At three o'clock in the morning, my mother heard a soft rapping on her trailer door. When she opened it, Waco, hat in hand, said, "He won't bother you again, darlin'."

"Where is he?"

"Right now I suspect the coyotes are having a feast. Does that bother you?"

"I hope he doesn't make them sick," my mother said.

## CHAPTER EIGHTEEN

## Pickled Punk

Because I managed Warbling Brothers Road Show and Circus, I was always getting calls from old man Warbling telling me he had added this act or that act. Some of them like Benji the Wolf Boy paid off in big dividends, but more often they flopped like dying fish, so bad the rubes laughed them off the stage. Herman the Human Worm and Gilda the Bat Lady were two such losers, but believe me, there were dozens of others.

So on a Thursday evening after we set up outside Escondido, I phoned the old man, and he told me he hired this woman, Lily Rosebaum. "And believe me, you ain't seen nothing like her."

I'd heard that before, but I learned long ago you didn't argue with the old man after he made up his mind. "When can I expect this treasure?" I asked.

"She's already there. Got a room at the Savoy Hotel. You go see her tonight, you hear? I told her to expect you."

"And just what does this Lily Rosebaum do? She's not another damn fortune teller, is she? You know how I feel about fortune tellers."

"Do?" He uttered a laugh. "She don't do nothing, but you'll find a place for her."

"And if she don't work out?"

"You've gotten rid of my mistakes before. You can get rid of this one if she flops. But she ain't going to flop."

Either from the old man hanging up or a bad connection, the line went dead, and our conversation ended. All I had to do now was go see this Lily and figure where I was suppose to put her. The old man hadn't been too exact on that point. I figured maybe she was an old girlfriend he wanted to help. We could train her to run a few kids' rides or maybe to keep the books, an area in which I always needed help.

Anxious to get it over with, I walked a half mile back up the highway to the hotel. The dingy building sat next to an old movie theater, the one sheet out front advertising JUNGLE SIREN with a beautiful Ann Cario shown in a sarong and menaced by a leering gorilla with Buster Crabbe rushing to the rescue. At that moment I would rather have bought a ticket and seen the cheap film than meet another of the boss' acquisitions.

The lobby of the hotel smelled like popcorn, a gift from the theater next door. I asked the clerk, an old geaser with a bald pate, the room number of Lily Rosebaum. His brow wrinkled like he wanted to ask me a question. "224," he said.

He waited until I reached the stairs before he leaned across the counter and asked, "You know the lady?"

"Never met her," I said. "Something I should know?"

"Well, I was just wondering--" He must have figured he over stepped his bounds because he shook his head and said, "None of my business really."

I climbed the dark stairs, the banister slick, the varnish worn off long ago. In one of the rooms someone played a radio loud enough for me to hear: "Who knows what evil lurks in the hearts of men? The Shadows knows." A cackling laugh followed.

One of the lights upstairs was out, casting the hallway in murky shadows. After much searching, I found 224 at the far end, the brass numbers scratched and dented. I knocked. From inside, a woman said, "It's not locked."

I turned the knob and stepped into the room, darker than the hall, the only light coming from the hotel's neon sign attached to the front of the building. It took a moment for my eyes to adjust before I located her next to the window, a shadow nestled in a chair and facing me. A breeze, cold as death, pressed against my cheek. I won't say I was afraid, but this whole thing had turned spooky.

I reached behind me and slammed the door shut, the thin walls rattling with the impact. "All right, what the hell's going on here?"

"I like sitting in the dark. It comforts me," she said, her voice soft and throaty. "The light switch is on your right."

My fingers fumbled along the wall until I found the button and pushed it. The bulb couldn't have been more than 25 watts, but I could see her clear enough, and I still didn't know what the hell was going on.

She sat in a rocker, her legs crossed, and the little bit of calf and knee looked shapely enough. In addition, her black dress emphasized her thin waist and bosom. Perhaps her hips were a bit wide, but then I liked my women to have wide hips. All in all, I'd say she looked pretty good, except for the black veil that hid her face. At first glance, she reminded me of a book I read as a kid, SHE, where this gal wore a veil because her beauty was so great men fell in love with her the moment she allowed them to see her face.

"Lily Rosebaum?" The veil moved slightly as she nodded. "Mr. Warbling said I should find a place for you."

"Yes."

I glanced around the room, trying to take stock of who she was, but I saw nothing personal, nothing to give me a clue, except on the dresser sat a half-empty bottle of Jack Daniels. "So what's your shtick?" I asked, and when she failed to answer, I said, "You do know what we do, don't you? You know what kind if business I run?"

"I know."

"So what can you do? Where can we fit you in?"

"I have only this." She took the veil in both hands and pulled it up, exposing her face.

There's no way I can describe what I saw--I don't think anyone could, not if he knew all the words in the world. The best I can do is say her gray skin looked like wax that got too close to a fire so that all the features melted into something hardly recognizable as human. One eye dropped way below the other, her nose wandered down to her mouth, overlapping it, and her crooked and swollen lips ran northeast to southwest.

She showed the kindness to quickly drop the veil back in place.

I had lived the carny circuit long enough to believe myself immune to shock, but I wasn't prepared for what she had shown me. I tried to remain stoic, to show absolutely no emotion, and maybe I succeeded, maybe not, but my belly heaved and bile rose in my throat. It took a good long minute before I found my voice. "Yeah, I can find a place for you."

"Mr. Warbling said you would. It was great kindness on his part."

"Kindness has nothing to do with it. The old man sees you as an attraction. You're money to him."

With a shrug, she said, "I have nowhere else to go."

"Then you're going to be right at home with us. A lot of our people feel the same way."

"Do you accept them--I mean those like me?"

"Sure we do."

"I mean you, personally--do you accept them?"

"I'm the boss. They work for me. I tell people what to do, and they do it. Some I like, some I don't, just like any other business." I leveled a finger at her. "You follow orders, and we'll get along."

"You didn't answer my question."

"I only keep people around I trust. That's accepting them, isn't it? I want to be able to trust you."

"Like I said, I've got nowhere to go. I won't give you any trouble."

"That's what I like to hear."

She came the next morning, carrying one frayed and scratched suitcase. I was with Becky at the ticket booth counting out the change and handing her the tickets. I told her I might be expecting Lily, and sitting behind her cage, she saw her first. "I think that woman's here, Boss." As an after thought she added, "Somebody must have died."

I peered around the edge of the booth to see Lily still in her black dress and black veil. Her shoes stirred up small clouds of dust. I stepped out to meet her. "I got this guy who's going to see to you," I said.

I called Dali over. Earlier that morning I told him about Lily and asked him to take care of her. When she saw him shuffling toward us, she tensed like I insulted her. I could see why. After all, Dali was a hunchback with a nose spread all over his face and big, red lips like they were painted on. "Don't get you dander up. I'm not insulting you," I said. "I trust Dali with everything. Nobody works harder than the kid."

Her shoulders relaxed, and she allowed him to lead her away. Half an hour later, he found me setting up the booth where rubes throw softballs at bowling pins. "I got her a place. She's rooming with Ruby."

Ruby was the contortionist who could screw her body into a hundred impossible positions. She worked the freak show along with Benji the Wolf Boy and Vilma the Bearded Lady and Anatol the Three-Legged Man and Stacy the Half-Man, Half-Woman and Leon the Pin-Head and Chandra the Spider Woman. If anybody could handle living with Lily, it was Ruby.

"Did you see her face?" I asked.
"The wind lifted the veil. I saw enough."
"The old man thinks she'll be a big hit."
"You going to set her up as one of the main acts?"
"I'm thinking of making her our pickled punk."
His brow raised in genuine surprise.

A pickled punk was an annex attraction where, after the regular acts, a barker offered the rubes a special attraction behind a curtain where they could see for only an additional twenty-five cents, a mere two bits, one of the most startling, unforgettable sights they were ever likely to see. Ours was a two-headed baby in a jar of formaldehyde. Of course, it wasn't real--we bought the exhibit from a company in Cincinnati--but it looked real enough to the rubes.

"A live pickled punk? I ain't never heard of such a thing," Dali said.

"That's the beauty of it," I said. "She ain't a fake. This is the way I see it happening. As the rubes pay their money and crowd in, the area is dark. Just a light on Lily. She's wearing that black dress and maybe showing a little leg, maybe a little cleavage. We give the rubes a sob story that builds to the moment when she lifts the veil. Just for a couple of seconds, enough for them to catch a glimpse of that face. Then the curtain falls, the lights come up." I laughed. "That ought to give them the shock of their lives. It'll scare the living bejesus out of them."

Doubt clouded Dali's face, and I said, "You don't think it'll work? Hell, I thought it was a damn fine idea."

"It sounds great, Boss."
"But--" I said.
"She doesn't seem all that scary to me. I don't think she'll scare anybody."

"We'll see about that," I said. "I've got plans--big plans. And I think the old man was right for once. She's going to be a moneymaker."

"Maybe so," he said, but he still didn't sound convinced.

So we stored the fake two-headed baby in one of the trucks and installed Lily Rosebaum as our pickled punk. At the first show, I watched while our man gave his spiel about the extra-special attraction behind the curtain and the rubes part with their coin and rush in. I waited outside--after all, I had seen her face once. I didn't need to see it again. The moment Lily lifted her veil, I heard the gasps and screams. As the rubes exited, I studied their blood-drained, stricken faces, the shock of Lily following them all the way out on to the midway. Her image would stick with them the rest of their lives.

Dali had been wrong about Lily. He thought she would flop as an attraction, but she proved to be one of the best draws we ever had.

I had been wrong about her, too.

Back in '46 I had seen a film called THE BRUTE MAN starring this guy Rondo Hatton. As a young man, he had been tall and good-looking, even voted the 'most handsome' by his high school classmates, but as an adult, a disease called acromegaly disfigured him so badly he could only play monsters in movies. When I first hired Lily, I saw her as the female equivalent of Rondo Hatton. Once people looked upon that grotesque face, that crumpled flesh, they would see a monster right out of a Universal horror movie.

The fear she inspired was far different than I anticipated. People didn't see her as a creature they feared. Instead they saw her and said to themselves: That could've been me. And that fear proved far more powerful than the one I envisioned.

One afternoon between towns, we camped on the outskirts of Palm Springs. By then Lily had been with us for almost a month. I had kept my distance, mainly because I dreaded talking to her. I didn't know what to say. She seemed so different, so less accessible than any of the others that I had to force myself to go to her.

I found her in the trailer alone, her back to the door, a book in her lap, and on the small table at her hand, a glass with an half-inch of Jack Daniels. She lowered the veil and faced me, but not before I caught a glimpse of her chin, which looked more like a series of raised blisters that had scabbed over. "I just came by to see how you've settled in," I said.

"I'm fine. No use to trouble yourself." She slurred her words.

"I know it's hard to adjust to this kind of life," I said. "If you need anything--"

"What I need, you haven't got."

"Still--"

"I just want to be left alone," she said.

So I left her alone, as did most of the performers and crew. Even Ruby, her roommate, left her alone, so that Lily spent most of her free time in the trailer, reading books and getting drunk.

Yet in all the years that have passed since then, seldom a day passes that I don't think of her. It doesn't take much. It's always a woman who brings her back--the inflexion of a word, the shape of a wrist, the shadow of a mole, a tuff of loose hair-- and suddenly she is right before me.

At first, I didn't understand why I couldn't put her out of my mind. I didn't brood over Benji the Wolf Boy or Leon the Pin Head or Chandra the Spider Woman or any of the others. So why Lily?

Dali was the one who explained it to me. One evening the two of us were at the pie wagon having dinner when Lily passed on the way to her trailer. She said nothing, and neither of us spoke to her. As a matter of plain fact, I kept my eyes glued to the plate, hoping she wouldn't say anything.

After she was gone, Dali said, "She is great box-office, Boss."

"The ugliest woman in the world. Hell, the ugliest person in the world. How could she miss?" I shook my head. "But do you know what don't make one bit of sense? I've seen some people come back three and four times--paying good money--just to get an another glimpse of her. What do you make of that?"

Dali scratched his chin, dried flakes peeling off and spotting the front of his shirt. When he spoke, his heavy bottom lip flapped like a lose tongue in a shoe. "She makes people feel better about themselves. Hell, she even makes me feel better about myself."

"What the hell you talking about, kid?" I asked.

"When people look at her, they see someone worse off then them. No matter what, their lives have to be better than hers. I mean, look at me, Boss. Who the hell am I? I'm close to a freak myself, ain't I? I got this hunchback, and my face ain't nothing to be proud of. People might stare at me, might even make fun of me, but if I had a face like hers--" He shrugged, the hunch on his back rolling like a boulder on its way downhill.

Lily's drinking grew worse, and it came the point you could smell it on her during her act. I cautioned her about it, and for a while she kept it hidden well enough so that I didn't have to say anything else. She lasted the rest of the year, then packed her one bag and left. She didn't say why, but she didn't have to. Some people just aren't cut out for carny life.

Afterward we unpacked the two-headed baby and restored it as our 'pickled punk.'

# CHAPTER NINETEEN

## Family Matters

I had an uneasy feeling when we pulled into San Oro, the last town on our schedule for the year. But I always had that feeling at the end of a long season just before we headed north for our winter quarters in Richmond. As a result, I dismissed my doubts as nothing more than stupid nerves.

San Oro was a small community just outside San Diego and perched right on the border. It boasted a population of five thousand, the majority of Mexican descent. A number of other small communities lay within a few miles, giving us a good base from which to draw customers. We had played San Oro twice since I had taken over as boss of Warbling Brothers Road Show and Circus, and I liked the town because, beyond a scuffle or two between drunks, we never had any problems there.

We set up in a large vacant area on the west edge of town. We picked the spot for the Ferris Wheel first so that it became the center of the midway, and I was looking over the ground when this Cadillac pulled up, dust from its wake rolling over us, and out stepped this guy wearing a Stetson and cowboy boots along with a suit and tie. He had a pair of cold blue eyes that looked through me all the way to the next county. He flipped back his coat to expose a badge pinned to his vest. "I'm Sheriff Beasley. You in charge here?"

"Our permits are in order," I said. "I can show you if you like."

"I'm not here about that." He glanced around at the seventeen trucks and the people standing around waiting for me to give orders. "You've got a big operation here."

"Ringling Brothers and Barnum and Bailey are big. We're a little outfit compared to them."

"You're big enough for San Oro." He wasn't any taller than me, but the way he stood, his legs slightly spread, his jaw tilted up, you could see he thought he owned the world. "You're going to have a lot of people here starting tomorrow. I figure three or four thousand a day."

I didn't have any idea where he was going with this, but I played it cagey. "You're overestimating. Trust me, we'll be damned lucky to draw two thousand for the whole weekend."

"Not going to argue the point." He reached into his coat pocket and drew out a pack of Luckies. "You're bound to attract trouble. You're going to need protection."

"When we were here last year we didn't have any trouble," I said.

"Things change. We've gotten a lot of riff-raff drifting into town lately, mostly from the other side of the border." He lit up and took a deep puff, letting the smoke drift out of his nose. He tossed the still lit match in clump of dry grass. We both stared as a small flame sprung to life before he ground it out with his boot. "Bad time of the year. Fire season."

"How much is this protection going to cost?"

He took a couple of puffs as he tried to figure how much he could soak us for. "You'll need at least two deputies full time. A hundred for each, another hundred for--" He paused while he tried to think of a suitable excuse. "--for personal incentives."

"That's pretty steep," I said.

"I could make it fifty percent of your gate." He took one long drag, the tip burning bright in the mid-morning sunlight, then he tossed the butt in the dirt. "Fortunately, I'm a reasonable guy. Three hundred cash. Payable in advance. That means right now."

I went to my trailer where I kept our receipts in a safe. Five minutes later I was back peeling off tens and twentys and laying them across his palm. He slipped the bills in his wallet.

He got back in his Cadillac and drove off. Up until then, the performers and crew stood around watching us, not exactly sure what was happening. I signaled them to unload. Mac asked me where I wanted the Ferris Wheel, and I started to tell him to put it any damn where he wanted, but there was no use taking it out on the him. Instead I pointed to a level spot in the center of the vacant lot. "That'll do," I said.

By six that evening, all our rides were up and ready as were the tents for the shows and the booths for games. Once I finished inspecting the midway and made it to the pie wagon, most of the workers and performers had eaten and taken themselves off to their trailers or sleeping quarters. Starting the next day--a Friday--we would have three eighteen hour days of non-stop work.

The only person still eating was Waco who, along with his granddaughter Lily, was one of the circus acts. Waco was an old cowboy who had ridden the trail herds before the turn of the century and knew a lot of the old timers like Wyatt Earp and Doc Halliday--or at least that was what he told us. He certainly looked the part, his face as wrinkled as a sand dune, his hair and beard as white as goose feathers.

After the cook filled my plate, I took a seat across from him, and Waco said, "That tinhorn sheriff is as crooked as a sidewinder."

"He's no worse than most."

He leveled his fork at me. "I'm telling you, Boss, that son-of-a-bitch is trouble. You watch out for him. I know what I'm talking about here."

"I know you do," I said.

Even before we opened the next day, the two deputies showed up. I was at the ticket booth passing Becky the cash box when their patrol car glided to a stop and the two climbed out. From a distance, they were mirror images of each other. Both stood just under six feet, and both had inflated bellies, but as they drew closer, I saw one was a good fifteen years older than the other, and he had a scar that ran from the corner of his left eye to the middle of his left cheek. I had dealt with plenty of ex-cons, and I could spot them a mile off. I think it was in the way they walked, their shoulders pushed back, their mouths curled up. Both these guys fit the bill.

The older cop was puffing on a big cigar, smoke swirling around his head like ground fog. Without taking the weed out of his mouth, he said, "I'm Fred. This is Frank."

"You guys don't have to stick around," I said. "You've been paid. Take the weekend off. We can handle things just fine."

The young cop snickered and shook his head. "Sheriff

sent us. We're staying."

I didn't like the idea of these two sticking around all weekend looking over our shoulders, but I saw right off there was no use arguing with them. "Suit yourself," I said.

They wandered off up the midway. I watched them until they stopped at one of food stands where they spoke to the girl behind the counter. A moment later she passed them a couple of hot dogs and beers. They walked on stuffing the food in their mouths.

At that point I went to find Dali. Now as you know, Dali was this hunchback kid who had been with Warbling Brothers for the past couple of years, and he was not only smart but a good worker, despite his condition. He was an all-around handy man, and when we needed a substitute for one of the game booths or to run a ride, he jumped right in. But today I had a different job for him. I found him at the Ferris Wheel with Mac, the two of them sitting on the ground drinking coffee and jawing.

"What's up, Boss?" Dali asked.

"You see those two cops I was talking to? Keep an eye on them."

Dali tossed out the dregs of his coffee and stood. In his socks he couldn't have been over five feet in height, and his nose wandered over half his face. He was ugly as hell, but there was no one I trusted more. "They do look like trouble, Boss."

"Trouble I don't need."

Less than half an hour later, the first customers arrived, and it didn't take long for the midway to fill. When the sun dipped low on the horizon and I still hadn't heard from Dali, I began to think my fears were groundless. I should have known better.

Just past six, Dali found me having supper at the pie wagon. "We got problems with Frick and Frack, Boss."

I threw my fork on the half-filled plate. "Tell me."

"About an hour ago, they pulled this high school kid off behind the trucks and slapped him around. They took his money and sent him running. At first I figured maybe he mouthed off or maybe they knew he was trouble."

"But you don't think so now," I said.

"They did the same to a second kid, then this older guy.

I saw them rough him up and empty the guy's wallet right in front of the guy's wife and kids. They was all Mexicans, and for all I know, they was all wetbacks." Dali shook his head, his wispy hair falling into his eyes so he had to brush it back. "That don't make it right. I tell you, Boss, it was raw."

"Go find Sean and Fergus," I said. "Have them meet me at the Ferris Wheel."

With a nod, Dali shuffled off to find the O'Malley brothers, fraternal twins who looked nothing alike except for their red hair. Sean stood a head shorter than me, but I'd never met a tougher guy pound for pound. On the other hand, Fergus was a head taller than me with the largest pair of hands I'd ever seen. Whenever I needed muscle, I called on them.

They were waiting for me. "You boys hang back. No threatening moves unless they start something."

"And if they start something?" Sean asked.

"Just don't kill 'em," I said.

Sean looked vaguely disappointed.

I found the two cops beside one of the food stands stuffing their faces with hotdogs and bottled beer. "You boys have been busy," I said.

The older one shrugged. "Just doing our job."

"Roughing up guys and taking their money ain't part of the job," I said. "You keep this up, word gets around, and pretty soon people will stop coming, and we won't have any customers. So you better hear what I'm telling you. You pull one more stunt like that and I'll close the show, pack up and leave. I'll pass the word around, and you'll never get another show of any kind to come to this jerkwater town."

The younger cop said, "They were only spics. There's no harm in that."

"Goddamnit, open your eyes," I said, my face suddenly flushed. "Most of this crowd is Mexicans. Those are our customers. If anybody is going to get their money, it's us, not you. Just leave them alone."

"Now see here, bub--" The older deputy poked me in the chest with enough force to send me back on my heels. "--you got nothing to say about what we do."

Sean and Fergus stood off to one side, and the cops never saw them. The brothers started forward, intent on breaking their skulls, but I shook my head. They backed off.

At that point I wasn't ready for a confrontation. Instead I went across the street to a phone booth and called Sheriff Beasley. I told him what the cops were doing. He laughed. "Like I said, we've had trouble from across the border. My boys are just keeping things in check."

Like I warned his deputies, I warned him that, if they kept it up, I would close down and leave town. They would never again see us or any other show. "I'll be right there," he said.

Five minutes later the Cadillac roared into the parking area, the tires swirling dust and rocks. I stood by the entrance so the son-of-a-bitch would see me right off. He jumped out of the car, his face the color of red paint. He came right up to me so we faced each other eye to eye. "I don't like being threatened."

"Your deputies are driving away customers, and I'm losing money. We paid you for protection, and what we're getting ain't protection. Now rein in your boys or we'll get packing."

His eyes blazed and the veins on both temples beat furiously, but he must have seen the futility of arguing with me. If he expected any payoffs from us in the future, he would have to take care of things now. He stepped past me and went up the midway in search of his deputies. Half an hour later he found me in front of the circus tent as I watched customers buy tickets. By then he had calmed down. "I told them to mind their p's and q's. They'll do what they're told."

"I appreciate it," I said, and I meant it.

Inside the circus tent, our three-piece band struck the first notes that signaled the entrance of the ringmaster, and Beasley looked beyond me to the bannerlines. "Your show any good?" he asked.

"Come on in," I said. "Take a look for yourself."

We sat together high up in the bleachers. The show opened with the jugglers and closed with the high wire acts. In between the animal acts took center stage, the first of which was Waco and his horses. Over the years I had seen dozens of acts involving horses, acts like Texas Slim Gibbons and Cowgirl Millie Stone. None compared to Waco. As old as he was, he exerted less energy than any performer on the circuit. He carried a whip, but he never used it, not once, except to gesture this way or that, and the horses obeyed his every command as if they all shared some psychic connection.

Waco's act also included his granddaughter, billed as Lily Devine, a kid barely twenty, although she had a kid herself courtesy of some reprobate back in LA. She was a beautiful young woman, slender and round at the same time, with a face that reminded audiences of a young and more vulnerable Lana Turner. Graceful and athletic, she rode as if she were part of the horses themselves, and even though it was Waco's act, it was Lily who the audiences watched with fascination.

And it was on her that Sheriff Beasley fixed his gaze. "What's her name?" he asked. I told him, and he said, "I want to meet her."

I blanched at the thought of introducing him to the girl, but I had no choice. I had pushed the sheriff as far as I could, and if I denied him this request, he could make life difficult for all of us. Anyway, I reasoned, what harm could it do? "Sure," I said. "After the show."

After the last act, all the performers paraded around the ring to a rousing rendition of "The Aviators" by John Philip Souza. Sheriff Beasley and I waited until the stands cleared, then I led him to the dressing rooms, which were only flaps over areas where the performers could change. I called out to Lily that someone wanted to meet her, and she told us to come in.

She sat before a mirror, a jar of cold cream open on the table, but she had not yet begun to remove her makeup. She had taken the clip from her hair, which cascaded over her bare shoulders like Champaign. From the stands you could tell she was a good-looking woman, but up close, she took your breath away. Earlier I said she looked like a young Lana Turner, but in reality she was better looking, softer, her curves rounder, her legs long and slender, and when she smiled, she looked as innocent as the Virgin Mary. Of course she was no virgin. Her two-year-old son Cliff sat at her feet rolling a toy car in the sawdust.

Lily stood, and Beasley removed his Stetson, holding in his left hand while he extended his right. "That was quite a show you put on." She took his hand, and he didn't let go. "Maybe you and me could have a little drink. Maybe a late dinner."

She smiled politely and with some effort, slid her hand free. "Thank you, but I need to spend time with my son. I haven't seen him at all today."

That was one of the things I liked about Lily. Not only was she a down right gorgeous, she had a quick mind.

Beasley rubbed his chin, his eyes running up and down her body. I began to wonder if he was going to insist she have that drink, and if he did, what would I do? Finally he smiled and flopped his Stetson back on his head. "Maybe another time."

Lily returned his smile but offered no other encouragement. Beasley turned abruptly and stepped passed me. I watched until he disappeared out the front of the circus top.

I started to leave, too, when Lily said, "Why did you bring him back here?"

"He twisted my arm."

"He's a creep," she said. "Keep him away from me."

"Sure thing."

The next day proved no different from most Saturdays, except for the presence of Beasley's watchdogs who hovered around the midway like hungry lions. The midway filled early, the rides ran at near capacity for most of the day, and the rubes flocked to the game booths trying to win prizes. The circus played its one o'clock show to a packed house, the freak top drew its usual crowd of gawkers, and the hoochie koochie brought in scores of guys to see the girls in skimpy costumes gyrate their pelvises. All in all it was a profitable day, I had no complaints.

The last performance of the circus started at 7:30, and lasted a little under 90 minutes. By then I was at the opposite end of the midway dealing with a rube complaining about a couple of cops who had taken his wallet. The rube was Mexican of course, whose accent was so thick I had trouble understanding him. Behind him stood a heavy-set brown woman in a gray dress with a scarf wrapped around her head and young wide-eyed girl who clutched her mother's skirts. "I'll see what I can do," I told the man. "But they're cops. We don't have control over them."

I found Dali working the baseball booth. Two teenage

boys were tossing balls at the bowling pins, trying to impress the girls who stood to one side watching, and I motioned to Dali, who came down to the end of the counter. "Have you seen those two cops?"

"Fifteen or twenty minute ago that sheriff showed up with Frick and Frack, and they all headed toward the circus top." His brow wrinkled in worry. "What's going on, Boss?"

A knot of dread formed in my belly. I turned and sprinted to the rear of the circus top. I should have had Dali fetch the O'Malley Brothers, but I was so worried, I simply forgot. Or maybe I was stupid enough to think I could handle the problem on my own. The moment I entered, I discovered the two cops blocking entrance to Lily's dressing area, the younger one holding Lily's boy in his arms. Cliff was crying, and the cop was jiggling him and telling him to be quiet.

"What the hell's going on?" I asked.

A dirty smile twisted the corners of the older cop's mouth. "The sheriff is having himself a party. He don't want to be disturbed."

From behind the flaps of Lily's dressing room came the sounds of a struggle, and I started to push past when the night stick came out of nowhere and slammed against the side on my head. I lay in the sawdust, the world spinning away and turning black, and all the time Lily's kid was crying. I wanted to tell him to shut up, at least until the pain in my head went away. Forcing myself to my elbows, I tried to sit up, but the older cop put a foot in my chest and pushed me back. "I told you. He don't want to be disturbed. Now stay down unless you want another taste of the stick."

By then others had come into the top. My eyes were open, but I had trouble focusing, and my head felt as if it were about to roll off my shoulders. Waco burst in, and jumped at the two cops, and the older cop belted him with the night stick, too, the sound loud like splitting timber. The old man dropped in a heap, blood streaming down his face like water from a busted faucet.

A dozen of us were there by then, and all were angered by what they had seen. They surged forward as one, their faces twisted in murderous rage. Everybody loved Waco and Lily. The older cop drew his .38. The young cop dropped the boy and drew his weapon, too. I lifted a hand and waved my people back. At that point the cops and I both knew the situation had turned critical, and they were ready to start blasting. All it would take was one precipitous shout, one precipitous movement, and dead bodies would litter the sawdust.

Then the flaps parted, and Sheriff Beasley stepped out, his fingers fiddling with the top buttons of his shirt. His face was flushed, and his slick hair fell from under his Stetson and across his forehead. Unconcerned he faced the angry crowd. "Trouble starts and a lot of people will get hurt. Maybe even the kid here." He waved a thumb at Cliff who sat in the sawdust, his wailing temporarily calmed. Beasley told the cops to get me to my feet. "He can escort us out."

They grabbed me under my arms and dragged me along, their guns still drawn, and my people parted. Outside in the fresh air, I got my feet under me and managed to walk on my own, but the two cops kept tight grips until we reached the parking area. The sheriff gave them a signal, and they released me. I swayed a bit, but I could stand without their help. "Didn't mean for it to happen," Beasley said. "It's just that she got under my skin the first moment I saw her. I couldn't take my mind off her. She's damned fine, I can tell you that."

I touched the side of my head where a knot sprouted like a hard-boiled egg, but I kept my mouth shut. He said, "Probably best for all concerned if you close down and get the hell out of here. Otherwise--"

The three of them climbed in their black and white and roared off into the night, their tires kicking up rocks and dust. I stood there a while looking after them and waited for the pounding in my head to stop. Dali found me. "You okay, Boss?"

Together we walked back to the circus top where a crowd gathered in Lily's dressing area. Lily sat clutching a dressing robe at her neck, a bruise discoloring her left cheek. She sat stiffly, her eyes pinched and hard. Waco lay on a cot, his head propped up on a pillow, his eyes open but glassy. Bright blood matted his white hair and beard.

As I entered, Lily said, "Look what they did to Waco."

"Here's the deal," I said. My voice sounded husky and strained. "We try anything, and some of are going to get killed.

Do you want that?"
　　　She took only a moment before she shook her head.
　　　To Dali I said, "Start closing down the midway. Let's pack up and move out."
　　　The O'Malley Brothers were up front, their expressions saying they wanted action right then. If I had let them, I'm sure they would have hunted up those bastards, but what good would that have done, even if they had found them? Either the cops would be dead or broken or the boys would be. And even if the O'Malley brothers meted out punishment, they would be on the run the rest of their lives. I looked directly at them. "There's no arguing here."
　　　I felt the stirrings of resentment from everyone. They expected more out of me, some plan of revenge, some form of retribution, but I wouldn't let them sacrifice themselves for nothing. "Go on," I said, my tone suddenly harsh. "Stop lollygagging and just get it done."
　　　I helped Lily clean up Waco, washing the blood off his hair and face. The cut across the top of his forehead was long but shallow, and when I suggested we take him to a hospital, Waco muttered, "I ain't dying in no hospital. I'll stay right here, thank you."
　　　"You need stitches or that's going to scar," I said.
　　　"Think it will spoil my good looks? Hurt my chances with the ladies." His old, wrinkled face cracked a wry smile. "If I'd had my hogleg, I'd showed them bastards a thing or two. Maybe I will yet--" He closed his eyes and his voice turned sleepy. "--as soon I feel a little better."
　　　Lily looked across at me. "If he dies--"
　　　"Waco's a tough old coot," I said. "He's not going to die from a crack on the head."
　　　"That sheriff--"
　　　"He'll get his," I said. "I promise you."
　　　"Like you promised to keep him away from me."
　　　"I'm sorry, kid," I said. "I let you down. It won't happen again."
　　　We closed the booths first, then the rides, and soon the midway emptied even though it was barely ten. Ordinarily we would have had another couple of hours, maybe more, to rake in the change, but at that point, none of us cared. We worked

through most of the night, and just before dawn, rolled out of town.

We drove straight to San Diego where we camped in a large empty field near the railroad yards. The next day we were scheduled to load our trucks and performers on a special freight that would deliver us to Richmond. I spent most of that time trying to get over my headache.

I kept looking in on Waco and Lily. Despite what I told her, I was worried about the old man, and as soon as we settled in, I called a doctor we sometimes used when we were in the San Diego area, and he came and examined the old man. Afterward outside their trailer, he told me it was a concussion, a bad one, and that Waco should stay in bed for a few more days, at least until his vision cleared and the headaches went away. "I don't like the way he looks. It would be best if we moved him to the hospital."

"No chance there," I said.

When I asked about Lily, he said, "She's bruised, but no permanent damage--at least, not physically. And as for a possible pregnancy--that's not a worry. She just started her monthlies." He wore glasses that pinched his nose, and he removed them to wipe the lenses with his handkerchief. "I know you people don't like to call the police, but in this case--"

"It was a cop who did it to her," I said.

He slipped his frames back over his ears and looked at me through lens still streaked with dirt. "Then you'll get no satisfaction from that quarter," he said flatly.

I took out my wallet and peeled off twenty dollars that he tucked away in the breast pocket. He said, "We've known each other for what--ten or twelve years? Certainly since before the war, and you've always struck me as a level sort. I hope you won't do anything untoward at this point."

"We're headed north for winter quarters," I said. "That would seem to be the end of it."

He nodded. "In that case, I wish you the best. Perhaps we'll see each other next year."

"Maybe so." We shook hands, and hefting his bag, he walked off to his car.

On Monday morning, we loaded our packed vehicles, trailers and cages on flatbeds. The performers and workmen crowded into two passenger cars. I never heard anybody grumble, but I could see by their faces they were unhappy with me. I didn't blame them. They had every right.

Just before the train pulled out, I drew Dali aside. "You're in charge until I catch up."

He appeared surprised and a little worried. "Not a smart idea, Boss."

"No one ever accused me of being smart," I said.

Lily hung back so that she and her grandfather were the last to board. She heard me speak to Dali, and while the O'Malley brothers lifted Waco on the train, she said, "Are you doing this for me?"

"For you," I said, "and for Waco and for all of us. We're family. We take care of each other. I did a poor job of taking care of you. Now I need to set things right."

A vein in her temple beat furiously, and she said, "You're no knight in shining armor, no Sir Galahad. My honor doesn't need protecting."

"Sure it does," I said.

Five minutes later the train rumbled out of the yard, and I stood beside the tracks until the last car disappeared around a far curve. After that, I found a bar where I bought a beer and tried to think things through.

I stuck around San Diego for the next four or five days waiting for the swelling in my face to go down. During that time, I bought a used Ford sedan. I had enough money in my bank account so that I paid cash. Of course when the salesman filled out the papers, he asked for my driver's license, but like a lot of carny folk, not a few who were on the run for one thing or another, I owned fake ID's. I showed him one of those, but he didn't look at it too closely. When you pay cash, those guys don't ask too many questions. I also bought a couple of business suits and had a stack of business cards printed that read Anthony Harris, Investor, and under the name, an address and phone number in Dalhart, Texas. Of course neither existed.

I dyed my hair from light brown to full blonde, and with the addition of a fake mustache, I doubt my own mother, if she still lived, would have recognized me. I hardly recognized myself. By the time I checked out and headed back for San Oro, the knot on the side of my head had shrunk to the size of a black-eyed pea, and my hair hid it.

San Oro had only one hotel, a two story, red brick building, probably built before the First World War, the facade cracking and crumbling, the windows so dirty you wondered if they had been washed since the Depression. A mousy little man registered me, and I made a show of telling him I was moving my investment firm and looking for possible towns to relocate. San Oro was high on my list. He smiled and said how prosperous the town was, and he would be glad to help in any way he could.

My room, shabby and smelling of smoke, looked out on the sheriff's office directly across the street. I couldn't have gotten a better room if I had asked. For most of the first day I sat at my window and made mental notes. The sheriff came and went three times, twice with Frick and Frack, once without them, but when the day ended, he left alone.

The next evening, I followed at a distance until he reached his house, a dark one-story frame on the edge of town. It lay at the end of a dark street, surrounded by desert, dry and bare. A thick wire fence surrounded the property, and a large German Shepard greeted him at the gate. When he entered the house, he flicked on the light. I sat in the car half a block down, hidden within the shadows of a heavy pepper tree.

Around nine, a black Chevy pulled up before the house and a woman got out, smoothing her skirt as she approached the gate. The German Shepard growled, than began barking loud enough to wake the neighborhood if anybody had been asleep. The woman, a short, slim redhead, waited until Beasley came to the door and called the dog's name. It ceased its barking, and the woman entered the yard and went into the house. She stayed less than half an hour, came out, got in her car and drove away. Right after, the house went dark. The woman didn't return.

For four nights I watched Beasley's place, and he followed his routine like rote, although it wasn't always the same woman.

On the fifth night, I bought a pound of ground steak at the local grocery. Back in my hotel room, I took a carton of sleeping pills the doctor back in San Diego had given me, crushing them and mixing the powder in the meat.

Just before nine I drove out to Beasley's house, arriving

in time to see a woman enter, Beasley's hand patting her butt as he closed the door. Half an hour later, she left, Beasley extinguished the lights, and black shadows engulfed the cul-de-sac. I waited a full hour before I climbed out of the car. I approached the gate, the dog growled, and I tossed the meat into the yard. The animal never barked, not once. He caught the scent of the meat and went right for it, and by the time I got back to my car, he had devoured it.

After another twenty minutes, I went to the gate, opened it and entered the yard. The dog, stretched out on the front lawn, was barely breathing. I hoped I hadn't killed it, but if I had, chalk it up as an innocent casualty.

Keeping to the shadows, I made my way to the rear of the house. The only weapon I carried was a long bladed, serrated knife, one I bought at a pawn shop in San Diego. At the back door, I turned the knob, and the door opened. Too easy, I thought. He must have had some idea, some inkling of my presence, and set a trap. At this point, if I told you I wasn't scared, I'd be lying. I figured any moment Beasley was about to come out shooting.

I stood very still for a long time trying to control my breathing, and when nothing happened, I realized the bastard was so arrogant he never believed anyone would come after him, and he had grown careless. He thought himself invincible.

I stepped into the kitchen, my soft sole shoes soundless against the linoleum floor. I heard his snoring and followed it to the bedroom, deep in darkness. I waited just inside the doorway until I made out the figure lying on his back, his mouth agape.

As I leaned over the bed, I must have awakened him. His eyes opened, but before he could move, I covered his mouth and slid the knife across his throat, the sharp blade sinking deep, severing blood vessels and vocal cords. With one hand, he grasped the gaping cavern, trying to hold back the geyser of blood, and with the other, he fumbled under his pillow for a .38. He managed to lift the weapon only to have it slip away like mercury and tumble to the floor. He tried to speak, his lips quivering in wordless cries.

I drew up a chair and sat beside him. "Do you know who I am?" I asked. He shifted his frighten eyes to try to see my face. "You certainly remember the carnival and Lily. Now

I want you to listen carefully so you can understand what I'm going to tell you. When you did what you did to Lily, it was like you did it to my sister--or my daughter. We're carny, and carny are family, and family is the most important thing in the world."

He managed to hold on until I finished, and he heard what I had to say, although I don't know if he understood. He was too scared of dying.

I drove back to the hotel. The lobby was empty, and I made my way to my room without being seen. I washed up and changed clothes. Early in the morning, I simply walked out of the hotel, got in the car and drove north. On a deserted part of the highway, I tossed out a bundle out containing a suit spotted with blood, a knife wiped clean, a fake mustache and blonde hair dye. In Bakersfield, I found a used car lot and sold the Ford, losing a little over five hundred in the exchange. Afterward, I rented a room and dyed my hair back to its original color.

By eight that evening I was on a Trailways bus headed for the bay area. Only then did I allow myself to think about what I had done. I didn't exactly feel good about it, but I sure as hell didn't feel bad either. If I harbored any doubts at all, they lay in the fact that as carefully as I executed my plan, I figured that someday, perhaps in the very near future, a black and white might pull up at Warbling Brothers, and cops might haul me away to be fried up by the state. If that happened, so be it. Hell, given a second chance, I would have killed the bastard again. My only regret was that someone didn't do it before me, which would have saved me a whole lot of trouble and worry.

When I got to Richmond, I called Dali, and he picked me up at the bus station. He didn't ask me any questions. He knew better.

As soon as I reached the encampment, I went to find Lily and her grandfather. They were at the pie wagon having supper. Waco had the late edition of the Chronicle spread out before him. He folded the paper, and passing it to me, tapped an article that began on the front page. The headline read: 'San Oro Sheriff Murdered.' I read the first two paragraphs, which said an unknown assailant or assailants had poisoned the sheriff's watchdog, broken into his house and killed him. At present the authorities had no suspects but believed a gang from across the border responsible.

"I guess he got his," Lily said, "just like you said he would."

As the days turned into weeks, the weeks into months, the possibility of cops hauling me away receded further and further into the realm of the unlikely. I began to feel a sense of safety, even when we returned to San Oro a year later. By then the town had cleaned up its act, electing a couple of men to the city council whose names were Torres and Gomez. The cops paid us only one cursory visit to tell us to play by the rules. No brides, no threats, no trouble. While Frick and Frack still worked for the Sheriff's department--I saw them in town as they drove by--they stayed far away. Maybe they had cleaned up their act, too.

Or maybe they understood better than Beasley that if you hurt us, we hurt you. After all, a family takes care of its own.

END

CPSIA information can be obtained at www.ICGtesting.com
Printed in the USA
237893LV00001B/206/P